The
MAGICIAN'S
COMPANY

Also by Tom McGowen

The Magician's Apprentice
(the first book of Tigg's adventures)
The Time of the Forest

The
MAGICIAN'S
COMPANY
Tom McGowen

♦ ♦ ♦

LODESTAR BOOKS · E. P. Dutton · New York

Library of Congress Cataloging-in-Publication Data

McGowen, Tom.
   The magician's company/Tom McGowen.—1st ed.
      p.   cm.
   Summary: The magician Armindor and his young apprentice
Tigg return from the Wild Lands to warn the rest of the world
that intelligent ratlike creatures know as the reen lurk in
hiding in their cities, ready to rise up and destroy all humans.
Sequel to "The Magician's Apprentice."
   ISBN 0-525-67261-3
   [1. Fantasy.]   I. Title.   88-11107
PZ7.M16947Mag 1988   CIP
[Fic]—dc19   AC

Published in the United States
by E. P. Dutton, New York, N.Y.,
a division of NAL Penguin Inc.

Published simultaneously in Canada
by Fitzhenry & Whiteside Limited, Toronto

Editor: Rosemary Brosnan

Printed in the U.S.A.   W   First Edition
10 9 8 7 6 5 4 3 2 1

for Ross

Beneath a lead-colored sky that seemed ready to unleash a flood of rain at any moment, two figures on horseback, one leading a third horse piled with bundles, were trotting down a dirt road that ran through a flat, bleak countryside. The rider of the lead horse was a tall, big-bodied, elderly man with a round face and bald head that was surrounded by a fringe of white hair. He was dressed in a long-sleeved, sky blue robe and leather sandals—garb that marked him as one of the Guild of Sages, men and women who were devoted to solving the mysterious workings of the world and rediscovering the ancient magic that been lost to humankind for some three thousand years. The second rider was a boy, perhaps twelve years of age, with dark eyes and a thatch of curly black hair. He was dressed in a sleeveless smocklike garment of undyed cotton, which hung to his thighs and was belted with a length of twisted cloth. His legs and feet were bare. His skin, like that of the man, was a natural tan color, and this, together with the darkness of hair and eyes, showed that man and boy were natives of the southern part of their continent, although the country through which they rode was in the far north. The ears of both man and boy were pointed, faintly tubular, and capable of being tilted slightly forward or backward, but such ears would have caused no comment or notice, for they were like the ears of most other humans of the world at this time.

Perched on the boy's shoulder, holding onto his head with handlike paws, was a furry cat-size creature that somewhat resembled a small bear, but with a noticeably round skull and a distinct chin beneath its protruding muzzle. Most people of this time and place would have recognized it as one of the animals called grubbers, which were reputed to live in little underground communities and to be able to communicate with one another by means of a primitive language. The creature peered with bright intelligent eyes at the bleak countryside through which it was passing.

The countryside was farmland, in the nation known as the Land of Wemms, but it was farmland that had been uncultivated for some time and had been largely taken over by fast-growing weeds that had obliterated the fields of grain and vegetables. From time to time the riders passed farmhouses with log walls and thatched roofs, but these were invariably empty and falling into disrepair. Sometimes they were merely blackened remains of a house that had been destroyed by fire.

"I guess they are still fighting their stupid civil war," observed the boy. He and the man had passed through this country some months earlier, finding that it was being torn by a conflict between the armies of two noblemen who both wanted to rule it. "That's too bad.

They'll be too busy to listen to what you could tell them, Armindor."

"I am afraid you are right, Tigg," said the sage. "We'll just have to try to get through the poor cursed country without running into any trouble, and bring our news to Inbal first."

"No hyoo-mens anywhere near here," remarked the grubber, Reepah, from Tigg's shouder. "Not even dead hyoo-mens. No smell in air."

After a time the sky could no longer hold the gathered moisture, and it began to fall in a steady soaking drizzle. The sage and the boy turned the horses off the road and sought shelter in a nearby abandoned farmhouse. "We may as well stop here for the night," suggested Armindor, the sage. "It will soon be dark anyway." They made a fire in the cellar, where it could not be seen from the outside, and over it they toasted chunks of grainy bread and heated a pot of spicy vegetable paste into which the bread was dipped.

The rain had ended by morning, and they continued on their way. Near midmorning they passed a crossing where another road came curving out of the distance, joining the road they were on at a right angle. They paused and scanned this road and the road ahead carefully before continuing, looking for a cloud of dust or any other sign of horsemen, for they did not want to be caught by a cavalry patrol of either of the two warring armies. There seemed to be no living thing near, human or animal, so they went on. But some time later the grubber, which had been dozing on the boy's shoulder, came alert and began testing the air with quivering nostrils.

"Death ahead," he said. "Dead hyoo-mens."

Armindor sighed. "I suppose there has been a battle somewhere ahead. Well, dead soldiers won't trouble us."

After a time they could see flights of carrion crows and daybats circling in the air ahead, over the road, and Tigg's sharp young eyes made out a large object standing motionless on the road. Drawing nearer, they saw that it was a four-wheeled wagon of the sort commonly used by traveling merchants, entertainers, healers, and such-like—stoutly built, spacious, and covered with a high pitched roof. It was gaudily painted with crude grinning faces, somewhat worn and peeling, which indicated that its owners were entertainers of some sort. But it was apparently empty, and the beast that had pulled it had been taken out of the harness and was gone.

Drawing abreast of the wagon, the horses suddenly snorted and shied, and the man and boy struggled for a moment to get them back under control. "There," said Reepah, pointing to the side of the road where lay the reason for the horses' excitement: three dead bodies. The bodies were those of a middle-aged man and two middle-aged women. The man and one woman had obviously been speared through the heart, the other woman's head was split by a terrible gash made by a battle-axe.

"Civilians," said Armindor sadly, surveying them. "I guess they encountered a cavalry patrol that decided they were loyal to the wrong side."

"Someone laid them out, though," Tigg pointed out. The three lay side by side, with eyes closed and their hands arranged on their chests, palms down, in the funeral style of followers of the god Garmood. "Soldiers wouldn't have bothered to do that."

"That's true," Armindor acknowledged. He glanced

about. "There must have been a survivor then. Someone who managed to hide from the soldiers and laid out these three when the soldiers left. Reepah, is there anyone nearby?"

The grubber lifted his snout. "Not near," he said after a moment. "Far ahead, maybe."

Armindor squinted, peering up the road, but there was no one in sight. "Well, perhaps we shall overtake whoever it is, in time. Let's be off. May the god these people worshiped be kind to their spirits."

The sage was right; they did overtake the survivor, as he had thought they might, about a day and a half later. They became aware of a solitary figure trudging along on the road ahead of them, and when they drew near enough they saw it was a young girl no more than Tigg's age. She wore a girl's typical sleeveless dresslike garment that hung to the calves of her legs, and like Tigg she was barefoot. A rolled blanket was slung over one shoulder, a leather watersack hung by thongs from the other shoulder, and she carried a bulging bag formed from another blanket with its four corners tied together. At the sound of horses' hoofs coming up behind her, she whirled and looked at them with an expression of terror. She had northern coloring: orange-blond hair, sky-colored eyes, and pale skin, with a scattering of golden freckles across her nose and cheeks, which appeared to be tearstained. When she saw that the riders were an old man and a boy, the terror left her face, and after staring at them for a moment, she turned back and resumed her progress on the road. She was limping noticeably.

Armindor slowed his horse to a walk and Tigg followed suit. In a moment or two the sage was abreast of the girl and staring down at her. He cleared his throat. "Young Maid," he said, using the formal address of an older person to a young girl, "do you live around here?"

"No," she answered curtly, not looking up.

"Ah," said Armindor. "Well, we passed an entertainer's wagon standing in the road yesterday, and—"

The girl stopped dead in her tracks and sank slowly to her knees. A long wailing howl of what sounded like mixed grief, rage, and protest tore from her throat, and her body began to jerk with racking sobs. Armindor reined his horse to a stop, as did Tigg behind him, and watched the weeping girl with sorrowful eyes. The boy watched her too, his young face grim.

After a time, her body quivering, the girl sobbed out her story, as if the telling of it would cleanse her of pain.

2

Her name was Jilla. She had been a member of a little group of traveling puppeteers that was trying to get out of war-torn Wemms and head for the Free City of Inbal, on the distant coast. They had stopped for a quick meal on the road three days ago and while eating had seen a cavalry patrol in the distance, heading toward them.

Hemm, the man who led the group, had told Jilla to hide. It was well known that soldiers of both armies often carried off girls, even girls as young as Jilla. The puppeteers' wagon had a concealed compartment beneath its floor, a space in which valuables could be hidden and which was roomy enough for Jilla to lie flat in. She had hidden herself away several times already during their journey.

Jilla had wriggled into the space and lain there in total darkness, all sounds from the outside muffled. She lay quietly, hoping the cavalrymen would simply ride on by, and that in a few moments the concealed entrance to the compartment would be lifted and she'd hear Hemm's voice telling her to come back out.

But that had not happened. She had heard shouting. Shortly, the wagon began to sway and there were heavy clumpings and creakings right above her. She guessed that several people had climbed into the wagon and were moving about in it. Soldiers, looking for something to steal, she thought bitterly.

The creakings and clumpings had continued for a time, then the wagon swayed again and there was silence overhead. Jilla heard the thudding of horses' hoofs, quickly fading away. There was total silence. She waited for Hemm to tell her to come out.

Time passed. She waited a while longer, fear and uncertainty growing. At last she could stand it no longer— she had to know what had happened. She wriggled until her feet bumped against the concealed entrance, pushing it open, and kept wriggling until she could arch her body forward and drop to the ground between the wagon's rear wheels.

She saw Hemm at once. He was lying face up in the road, no more than a half a dozen steps from where she stood. His mouth was open, his eyes stared unblinkingly, and the front of his gray smock was soaked with blood. He was clearly dead.

There had been a sudden, whispering roar in Jilla's ears, like the sound of the sea heard from a great distance. She took a couple of stumbling steps out away from the end of the wagon and stared about, knowing all too well what she would see. Yes, there was Ola's body slumped against one of the front wheels, and Anjin was a few paces from her, sprawled motionless in the road.

Jilla had never known her parents; they had died of

some sickness when she was a baby, but Ola was her aunt, and she had been reared and cared for by these three people. Her first conscious memories were of riding in the wagon with the three of them as they traveled from place to place to put on the puppet shows with which they made their living. The wagon, the two women, and the man had been her whole world for as long as she could remember. Now, everything she loved, everything that meant happiness and comfort and safety, the only things in the world that had been truly hers, had been suddenly torn away from her.

Jilla had no idea how long she knelt there crying. But finally, with eyes sand dry and burning and throat choked with pain, she lifted her head and thought about what she should do. What she wanted to do was to die herself, for there didn't seem to be any reason to go on living. But she couldn't think of any way to make herself die quickly; she had no weapon. She wished that the soldiers had discovered her and killed her, too.

Then she had found herself thinking of Ola, and of something Ola had told her once. "There'll be hard times as you go through life, dear," the woman had said. "Lots of 'em. There'll be times when you'll want to just give up and die! But you mustn't ever give up, Jilla. Because no matter how bad things may be, they'll usually turn good again in time, and when things are good it's worth being alive."

She had turned Ola's words over in her mind, and a sudden resolve had filled her. I won't give up, she had told herself fiercely. I'll stay alive!

She decided the thing to do was to keep on going to Inbal. She would have to do it alone now, of course, and on foot, because the soldiers had unharnessed the hornbeast that was drawing the wagon and taken it with them. But do it she would! She would survive by giving puppet shows by herself; she had been taking part in the puppet plays given by Hemm and the two women since she was eight years old, and she knew all the roles and stories by heart.

She climbed into the wagon and looked around. The marauding soldiers had left things in a shambles, but to her relief the puppets were undamaged. She spread a blanket on the floor and piled them on it—Giggle, the clown; Nasty, the evil one; Fatsy, the merchant; Arquipan, the sage; and Beauty and Hero. The soldiers had taken most of the food, but she found half a loaf of bread and the watersack, which was nearly full. She put the bread with the puppets and added a few other needs— cooking pot, stone-and-metal sparkmaker for starting fires, and a prayer stick. She gathered the ends of the blanket together and tied them to one another to form a bag. She rolled up another blanket and slung it over her shoulder, tying the ends together at her hip. She hung the watersack from the other shoulder. Holding the bag, she clambered back down out of the wagon.

Now came the moment she had been dreading. Putting the bag on the ground, she attended to the remains of her loved ones. Crying bitterly, she dragged the three limp forms to the side of the road, one after another, so they lay side by side. She closed their sightless eyes and arranged their arms so that their hands were on their chests. She kissed each of them for the last time, asked their spirits to watch over her, and bade each good-bye.

Then, her eyes swimming and her body shaking with

sobs, she had gathered up the sack and began determinedly marching up the road that led out of the hateful Land of Wemms.

The first three days of her journey had been horrible. Thoughts of Ola, Hemm, and Anjin were constantly on her mind, and she was tortured by grief. The journey itself was physically hard as well, for Jilla had never walked such enormous distances as she was now doing each day, and her feet and legs began to hurt steadily. Her stomach hurt, too, because she was trying to get by on no more than a bite or two of bread and a swallow of water each day, to make her provisions last.

Nights were particularly bad, for then she was bothered not only by grief and hunger, but also by fear. She had always slept in the wagon with three adults, and to now have to sleep alone in the open, surrounded by utter blackness, was terrifying. She knew that not only were there possibly large, dangerous animals prowling through the open countryside, but also supernatural beings—deadwalkers that ate people, hate-filled spirits, and other things. When night came she would lie shivering at the edge of the road, clutching the prayer stick and hoping nothing would notice her.

This morning, upon awakening, she had eaten the last of her bread, and she was hoping it wouldn't take much longer to get to Inbal or she might starve. The watersack was nearly empty, too. But she would survive, somehow. She was determined to!

When the girl finished her story and fell silent, Armindor heaved a deep sigh. Tigg watched him, a gentle smile curving the boy's mouth. He knew that Armindor, if he could, would adopt every orphan, waif, and poverty-crushed child in the world, and the sage would no more be able to keep from trying to help this utterly forsaken girl than he would be able to stop eating.

"Young Maid," said Armindor, "it is really quite a long way to Inbal, and I noticed that you are limping. We are headed for Inbal, too, so why don't you ride there with us? There's room for you on my apprentice's mount, and we can put your belongings on the packhorse."

She stared up at him, a sudden flood of renewed hope showing clearly in her expression. "Oh, thank you, Your Wisdom," she said, employing the polite form of address one used when speaking to a sage.

"I am called Armindor—Armindor the Magician," he told her. He pointed at the boy. "That is Tigg, my apprentice." He raised the hand higher to indicate the grubber on Tigg's shoulder. "And that is Reepah. Tigg, put her things on the packhorse."

The boy slid from his horse and approached Jilla to take the makeshift bag and watersack and blanket from her. He secured them among the bundles on the packhorse, then climbed back onto his mount and reached a hand down to help the girl scramble up behind him. In a few moments the horses were once more plodding on their way, and Jilla, holding onto the boy's sash, sensuously wiggled her toes and luxuriated in the delight of not having to use her feet anymore.

Tigg half-turned toward her. "Is Wemms your homeland?"

"No," she replied, her voice dripping disgust at the thought of being a native of such a vile place. "We traveled through the whole northland. We got caught in Wemms when the war started and we were trying to get out when—when—" She couldn't go on, a lump had come into her throat. She changed the subject. "Why are you in this awful place?"

"We're just passing through," he told her. "We've come from the Wild Lands."

Jilla gasped and leaned to one side, peering at his face to see if he was joking. But she saw that his expression was quite serious and she felt he was telling the truth. She was astounded.

The Land of Wemms was the northernmost point of the civilized part of the continent. Beyond it lay a vast unknown wilderness known as the Wild Lands, where no humans lived and which was generally shunned by everyone. It was the subject of scores of weird tales and frightening legends. It was said to be an abode of fearsome monsters and supernatural creatures, where poisonous mists seeped out of the ground, and the very rains that fell were searing venom that could blister the flesh off a person's body! There, in the midst of deep forests and fetid swamps, lay incredibly ancient ruins that glowed in the dark with an eerie green light, and were a person to set foot in them he would instantly become a blackened, shriveled corpse! The girl had never heard of anyone going into the Wild Lands for any reason, but this boy was saying, quite matter-of-factly, that he and the sage had been there!

"Why were you in the Wild Lands?" she asked in astonishment.

"We were looking for something," Tigg replied. He turned to look her full in the face. "The Wild Lands aren't really as bad as most people think. There *are* dangerous things there, and you do have to be careful, but mostly it's just fields and forests full of harmless birds and animals. All—well, most—of the terrible stories you hear about it aren't really true."

This was a revelation to Jilla, and she wasn't sure whether to believe it or not. But if Tigg had been there, he ought to know, she decided.

"What were you looking for there?" she asked.

"Armindor had learned of a place where there were supposed to be a lot of magical treasures left over from the Age of Magic. We found it—an ancient, ruined place. There *were* some old magical things there. Not as much as we'd hope for, but some wonderful things anyway." He jerked his head at the bundle-bedecked horse plodding along behind them. "They're in some of the bundles on the packhorse, along with—some other things."

Jilla was enthralled. This was as incredible a tale as she had ever heard a professional storyteller spin, as thrilling as the plots of some of the puppet plays she knew. The discovery of ancient magical treasures in an ages-old ruin in the Wild Lands!

"What are the magic things like?" she questioned. "What do they do?"

"One of them is a spell for far-seeing," he told her. "You look into it and it makes far things seem close. Another is a spell for cutting through cloth. The others—" He shrugged. "We don't know what they do yet. We have to study them and find out. That is a magician's main work, to find out about such things." There was pride in his voice.

"Are you taking them to Inbal to study?" Jilla asked him. "Do you live there? From the look and sound of you, I thought you must be from far in the south."

He grinned. "We are. Our home is the city of Ingar-

· 14 ·

ron, far beyond the Silver Sea. We'll go back there as soon as Armindor takes care of an important thing that must be done in Inbal."

"Are you related to the sage?" she asked.

Tigg shook his head. "I was a raggedy, half-starved orphan living in the streets of Ingarron," he confessed. "I slept wherever I could and I stole and picked people's pockets to stay alive! Armindor saved me from that— like he saved you from having to walk all the way to Inbal." He grinned. "He tricked me into becoming his apprentice, and at first I didn't want to be. Now I'm proud and happy that he picked *me* out of all the boys or girls he might have had!"

"He is a most kind man," murmured the girl, happily curling her toes again.

The grubber, who had been studying her intently all this time, now spoke in his squeaky voice. "You have little spots on face. Tick do not have spots. What are they for?"

The girl nearly fell off the horse. "It can talk! Did you teach it to say that?"

The boy was grinning again. "No. I taught Reepah to speak our language, but he decides what he wants to say. Grubbers can think as well as we can. Reepah is as smart as any human." He twisted his head to look at the grubber. "I think he's curious about your freckles. Those little spots on her face are called freckles, Reepah. They're not *for* anything. They just *are*. Some people have them and some don't."

"Uk," said the grubber, apparently satisfied with this explanation. He wiggled himself into a more comfortable position on Tigg's shoulder, closed his eyes, and appeared to be trying to take a nap.

Jilla's mouth was hanging open. She closed it and considered things. A magician and his apprentice who had dared the dangers of the Wild Lands to search for a magical treasure, and a beast that could think and talk like a human—these were certainly strange and interesting companions she had fallen in with!

· · · 3 · · ·

The Free City of Inbal was the northernmost port on the Silver Sea. A bustling metropolis of nearly nine thousand people, it had the typical look of a far northern community; private dwellings and public buildings alike tended to be high, long, and narrow, with steeply slanted roofs that encouraged snow to slide off. Almost all structures were built of peeled logs of pine and birch that were sealed with a kind of varnish made chiefly of tree sap, which gave a pale orange cast to the white wood and imparted a bright, warm feeling to the entire city.

"The first thing we must do," said Armindor as they passed through the broad northern gate of the city wall, "is to find a decent guestinghouse to stay in. And then, Tigg, we must go to the Sages' Guildhall of Inbal and let the Brothers and Sisters know what we have found out. It would be helpful if you went there with us, Jilla, for we'll need help carrying things."

It had been decided, the previous day, that Jilla would stay with the magician and his apprentice a while longer before striking off by herself. Armindor had urged this, Tigg had enthusiastically seconded him, and Jilla, understanding full well that the magician was concerned about her and was trying to extend his kindness, agreed. Despite her original resolve to survive on her own, she was enough of a realist to know that a lone young girl would have a desperately hard time trying to make a living by giving puppet shows in the streets of a big city, and she was glad to be able to postpone the beginning of her efforts to do so. At the same time, she did not like taking charity from Armindor and giving nothing in return, and she was determined to pay him back somehow. She felt that she probably owed him her life, for the journey to Inbal had taken many more days from the point at which she had met the magician and his companions, and she knew she could never have made it on her own—she would have run out of food and water, begun to starve, and grown too weak to go on, if Armindor, Tigg, and Reepah hadn't come along.

The horses clop-clopped up several narrow dirt streets until they came abreast of a building from which jutted a signboard painted with the pictures of a plate of food, a bottle, and a sleeping mat, which indicated the place was a guestinghouse where travelers could buy meals and sleeping accommodations. Armindor reined in his horse, Tigg followed suit, and the tethered packhorse came to a stop when the two other horses did.

The magician eyed the building thoughtfully, then nodded. "Looks all right," he commented and eased himself down off his horse. "Tigg, you and Jilla watch the horses while I go in and find out if they can provide a room for us."

He entered the building and soon returned, followed

by a pair of burly young men who began to unload the packhorse. "We'll stay here," he told the boy and girl. "These men will see to the horses and take our baggage to the room. It's nearly noon, so let's have a bite to eat and then we'll go right to the Sages' Guildhall. It's not far from here."

Following a luncheon in the guestinghouse eating room they went to the living quarters Armindor had arranged for: a large, main-floor room with three sleeping mats, a table, and several stools. Their belongings had been piled in a corner, and Armindor separated two carefully wrapped bundles and a tightly tied bag from the rest.

"I'd best take this one," he said, bending down for the square-shaped bundle. "You two split up the others." He heaved the bundle to his shoulder. "By Roodemiss's eyebrows, that's heavy!"

Jilla picked up the bag, then paused, sniffing. "This stinks! What's in it?"

"Dead enemies," said Tigg. Jilla glanced at him, expecting to see a teasing smile on his lips, but his face was serious. "I'll take it," he offered. "You carry the other one."

With a distinct feeling of relief she let him take the smelly bag from her. The thought of what might be in it was disturbing. She knew, from things that Armindor, Tigg, and Reepah had said to one another at times, that something very frightening and serious had happened to them in the Wild Lands, and she gathered that they had brought back something connected to that occurrence. Presumably, it was in that bag. Well, apparently they were going to show the contents of the bag to the sages of Inbal, so she would get to see whatever it was— although she wasn't quite sure she wanted to!

"Let's go," said Armindor.

Tigg, with Reepah perched on one shoulder and the bag slung over the other, and Jilla, clutching a lumpy bundle with both arms, followed Armindor out into the street and trailed after him down a number of other streets until they found the Street of Sages and turned down it to head toward an impressive-looking building that dominated the ordinary dwellings on each side. Its main part, which covered nearly a third of the entire length of the street, was a vast rectangle of horizontal logs each thicker than a man's body, piled to form walls twice a tall man's height. Four enormously thick logs, set upright, formed the corners of the rectangle. They were intricately carved with an abstract pattern that suggested piles of clouds. From the top logs of the rectangle a thatched roof sloped slightly upward to the base of a second story: another log rectangle, but narrower and not as high as the first floor. From the top of this rose another thatched roof, ascending much more sharply and reaching a long, high peak that was decorated with a row of wooden triangles that formed a long jagged line against the sky. From one end of this line jutted a long pole, from which hung an enormous blue banner on which was painted a representation of a human eye. This caught Jilla's interest.

"What is the eye on the flag?" she questioned.

"It is the eye of Roodemiss, the god of sages," Armindor told her. "According to our lore, he was a great magician during the Age of Magic. It is said that, when he saw the world was going to be destroyed by the Fire from the Sky and all magic would be ended, he rose to the top of the sky in a great machine he had built and has stayed there ever since, looking down to see that all is well with those who seek to regain the lost magic of his day."

With Armindor in the lead, they entered a tiny alcove with a massive door at the end. A thick, braided leather cord, emerging from an opening in the wall, hung by the door, and Armindor reached out and gave this several yanks. With each yank they heard, faintly, the *tunk* of a mallet striking a hollow wooden-cylinder gong on the other side of the door.

A few moments passed, then the door was opened by a bearded young man in a blue robe. His eyes took in Armindor's own blue robe, then shifted upward and fixed on the tiny round blue stone earring that dangled from the older man's left ear. Immediately he bowed, touching his forehead with the back of his right hand, a token of deep respect. Jilla suddenly understood that Armindor was a person of considerable importance among sages.

"I am Armindor of Ingarron," said Armindor, inclining his head in recognition of the other's bow. "Are there any Master Sages in the guildhall at this moment?"

"High Master Tarbizon himself is here, High Master," said the young sage. "Do you wish me to summon him?"

"Tarbizon's here? That's good luck!" exulted Armindor. "He can help if anyone can! Yes, please tell him we're here."

They followed the young man into the building and found themselves in a long narrow hall, the walls and ceiling of which were formed of panels of pale wood intricately carved with designs of plant leaves, fruit, flowers, and crawling insects. Hundreds of thousands of tiny, smooth pebbles of all colors, set in mortar, formed the floor. With a grunt, Armindor heaved the bundle off his shoulder and stooped to place it by his feet. The young sage was hurrying down the hall, his sandals slapping on the pebbled floor. Near the far end of the hall he turned into an entrance and vanished from sight.

He reappeared only moments later, at the heels of another bearded sage. This man was much older, and his beard and shoulder-length hair were heavily shot with gray. He was a slim man with a fine-featured face, and as he drew nearer Jilla observed that he, too, had a tiny blue stone ball dangling from his left ear as Armindor did.

"High Master Armindor of Ingarron; High Master Tarbizon of Inbal," intoned the young sage.

But the two older men obviously knew each other. They smiled and touched palms. "Brother Armindor," said Tarbizon. "By the eye of Roodemiss, it's been ten years, hasn't it?"

"Eleven," said Armindor. "It's good to see you again, Brother."

Tarbizon cast an interested glance at the two children with their burdens, and the bundle on the floor at Armindor's feet. "A little more than a moon ago, I received a message from the Ingarron High Council. It told of a secret document that had been discovered, written by a long-dead sage, giving the location of a place somewhere in the Wild Lands in which there were spells that had somehow been preserved during the three thousand years since the Fire from the Sky ended the Age of Magic. It said that you had been appointed to go look for the place, Brother." He looked again at the bundles and bag. "Can I presume that you found it?"

"We found it," acknowledged Armindor. "And we have brought back some spells. I'll show them to you,

Brother Tarbizon; in fact, I want you to keep some of them here for a time. But that is not the main reason I came to you. You see, while in the Wild Lands we learned of something—a terrible, unsuspected danger that may break forth at any time and shatter our world, Tarbizon! I need your help to spread a warning!"

With two fingertips, Tarbizon stroked his beard and regarded Armindor thoughtfully. "Hmmm. You arouse my concern, Brother! Well, let us get out of this hallway and go to the Chamber of Consideration, where you can show me all these things." He gestured at the bundle on the floor. "Pick that up and spare High Master Armindor the pain of stooping for it, Florn," he said to the young sage, who obeyed instantly.

Tarbizon turned and led them up the hall and through an entrance into a large open room, the walls of which were entirely covered with wooden shelves loaded with an incredible array of objects, and interrupted only by a large stone fireplace in the center of one wall. A long wooden table with a number of stools arranged around it occupied the middle of the room. A blue cloth banner like the one outside the building hung motionless from the high, vaulted ceiling, its bottom edge exactly intersecting the center of the table.

At Armindor's gesture, Tigg, Jilla, and the young sage, Florn, deposited their bundles on the table. "Now, first," said Armindor, "some important introductions." He put a hand on Tigg's arm. "This is my apprentice, Tigg, without whom I would not have survived the journey to the Wild Lands. It was actually he who discovered the use of several of the spells we found. He has the makings of a great magician, Brother!"

Tarbizon extended his hand. "Greetings, Apprentice.

You are most fortunate to have a teacher such as High Master Armindor." Tigg touched palms with him, bowing.

"Next," said Armindor, indicating the grubber perched on Tigg's shoulder, "is Reepah of the weenitok folk, which we call grubbers. I do not want you to underestimate him, Brother. It has long been known that grubbers have a language of their own, and are intelligent, but I did not realize how intelligent until I came to know Reepah."

"I kiv you kreetings, hyoo-man," said Reepah squeakily.

Tarbizon looked startled. "Er—greetings to you," he said, staring at the furry creature. Two fingers came up to stroke his beard. "Remarkable." he murmured.

"And this is Jilla," said Armindor. "She met with misfortune in the war-torn Land of Wemms, and we are assisting her, for a time."

"Now." He stepped forward and began to unwrap one of the bundles, opening it to reveal a cluster of objects. He picked up one of these and put it in the center of the table. Tarbizon and Florn bent over it eagerly. The thing appreared to be a small round box made of a shiny red substance, but the top was transparent so that the bottom of the box was visible. On the bottom were inscribed a number of unknown symbols arranged in a circle, and in the center of the circle was a shiny bluish object resembling a slim knife blade. It spun and quivered like a living thing for a moment or two, but as the two Inbal sages peered at it in wonder it slowly subsided and came to a stop.

"We don't know what this spell is for, yet," said Armindor. "But I can tell you that no matter how much you jiggle the box or where you put it, that shiny thing in the middle always comes to a stop pointing in exactly the same direction! You can turn the box so that any one of the symbols will line up with the pointer thing, which doesn't seem to make much sense, but"—he grimaced ruefully—"as we well know, it would have made sense to the people of the Age of Magic, and might have been very important for them!"

He picked up another object. It was a small thin cylinder, apparently made of the same sort of stuff as the mysterious round box. Armindor gently tugged at one end and the cylinder suddenly doubled in length. "There is a slightly smaller cylinder inside the first one," he explained. "It is held in place somehow, and can be slid in and out." He demonstrated. "We know what this is. It is a Spell of Far-seeing. You point it at some distant thing, look into the small end of it, and you see the distant thing as if you were standing right beside it." He looked toward Tigg, and said with pride in his voice, "My apprentice discovered the working of this spell." Tigg grinned and hung his head in some embarrassment as the two Inbal sages looked at him, Tarbizon with a pleased smile and Florn with an expression of respect.

Armindor brought forth more objects of ancient magic. A cutting device that fitted into a person's fingers. A half oblong of metal that would, amazingly, pull other small metal objects toward itself across a distance of two finger-widths or more. A cylinder that blew out tiny puffs of wind when a rod sticking out of one end was pushed in and out. A pair of small hollow cones with dome-shaped removable tops that were pierced with numerous holes. One of the cones bore a symbol that looked somewhat like a wriggling snake (S), while the other had a symbol that was a straight line with a half circle joined to its upper portion (P).

The excitement of the Inbal sages grew as they examined each of these things; together with Armindor they were soon heatedly discussing the possible functions of these marvelous objects—which had once been nothing more than cheap toys and household items.

Jilla, standing with Tigg some distance from the table, couldn't repress a giggle. "I always thought sages were so sober and dignified," she confided in a whisper. "They're acting like little children on Garmood's Feast Day!"

Tigg smiled, "I suppose they are, but—don't you see, Jilla, those things *are* exciting! They're bits of magic from the time when people had magic for everything! They had spells for curing any kind of sickness, spells for making all the food they wanted, spells for talking to each other across great distances, spells for *flying!*" His eyes were shining. "But then the Fire from the Sky destroyed everything, and people had to live like animals for almost three thousand years. Armindor says we've started to climb back up a little, but we're still far below the people of the Age of Magic. But if we can learn to use these spells, and others that are sometimes found, maybe we can bring back a little of that wonderful time! Maybe we can make life better and easier for people now, as it was then. That's what all magicians dream of doing, and that's why these magicians are so excited about those things."

Jilla nodded thoughtfully. She could see that being a magician meant a great deal to the boy, and she was beginning to understand why.

Armindor had unwrapped the square-shaped bundle,

revealing a large, battered, discolored metal box. "We have no idea what is in this. As you see, it is sealed with one of the ancient metals." He touched the thick, lumpy gray strip that ran around all four sides. "I suspect it will take a lot of hard, careful work to get it open, and I plan to try opening it when I get back home to Ingarron and have plenty of time. But I ask that you hold it and some of the other things here for safekeeping, Brother Tarbizon, until we are ready to leave."

Tarbizon nodded. "Of course. We'll keep them in the Room of Valuables, under guard."

Armindor turned toward the bag, which still lay unopened. His expression was sober. "And now," he said, "we come to the main reason why I'm here, Brother Tarbizon. This is the other thing I told you of, which we learned about in the Wild Lands. Believe me, Brothers, when I tell you that it is the most deadly and dangerous thing the human race has faced since the time of the Fire from the Sky! It will wipe us all out, Tarbizon, unless we can do something about it!"

Jilla couldn't hold back a gasp of horror at the sight of the thing he took out of the bag and placed on the table. For a moment she thought it was a dead baby, then she noticed its snoutlike nose, the rounded ears high on its head, and its long thin tail, and realized it was some kind of animal. It was about the size of Reepah, and it was lying on its back, its hind legs stretched straight out as a human's legs would have been, one foreleg at its side and the other bent over its chest. The feet on the hind legs were like long, narrow human feet, and instead of paws its forelegs ended in slender, humanlike hands. But both its toes and fingers were tipped with black, needle-sharp claws. Its long mouth was curled up in a frozen snarl, revealing sharp, pointed teeth. To Jilla, the thing seemed like an odd mixture of human and rat! It had a shriveled, blackened appearance, and it stank with the odor of decay.

"I apologize for the smell," said Armindor. "We smoked the thing to preserve it, but it was killed many days ago and it is obviously beginning to rot."

Tarbizon considered the thing, frowning. "Is this an animal of the Wild Lands, Armindor? I have never seen anything like it. It looks somewhat like a kind of rat."

Armindor nodded. "I suppose the ancestors of these creatures were rats that were changed by the Fire from the Sky, or *mutated,* as the old writings say. But no, Tarbizon, they do not live in the Wild Lands. They live among *us,* in our towns and cities! There are probably many of them here in Inbal."

"I have never seen such a creature here," protested Florn, and he immediately looked apprehensive at having spoken.

"They keep well hidden," Armindor said. "They generally walk on two legs, as we do, but when they want to, they can get down and scurry about on all fours, and then they are easily mistaken for nothing more than very large rats. You have probably often seen them without noticing, Brother Florn. They have been hiding among us for many years without our knowing it!"

"How did you learn of this?" asked Tarbizon.

"*It told me,*" said Armindor, pointing at the dead creature. "They are intelligent, Tarbizon, as intelligent as humans! Like Reepah, they have learned our language. Let me tell you what happened in the Wild Lands; it is a long story, but I will make it short.

"Unknown to Tigg and me, we were trailed by some

of these things almost from the very beginning of our journey to the Wild Lands, for they had learned what we were trying to find and hoped we would lead them to it. When I located the place where the spells were buried, the creatures revealed themselves. They held me captive for a time, and it was then that their leader told me something of them. They call themselves reen, and they boast that they outnumber us greatly in all our towns and cities. They have spied on us, so they know all our ways and secrets." He leaned forward, resting the knuckles of his hands on the table, fixing the two Inbal sages with his gaze. "And they have a plan for us, Brothers. They plan someday to rise up, wipe us all out, and take over the world for themselves!"

Florn looked shocked, Tarbizon looked thoughtful. After a few moments, he spoke.

"It is most disquieting to think of creatures spying on us," he said. "But surely, we haven't much to fear from them. I mean, how dangerous can they really be?" He waved a hand at the dead reen. "It has claws and sharp teeth, but it's really too small to be much of a threat. I suppose a large crowd of the things could attack a lone man and do him serious injury, but—"

"They have weapons, Brother," Armindor interrupted. "I told you, they are as intelligent as we are. We can make weapons and so can they." He reached into the bag and brought forth a small wooden box, fastened to a loop of leather, and a thin tube made of bone, half as long as the dead reen's body. Tipping the box, Armindor shook out several tiny needle-pointed darts, also made of bone, with feather tufts at the ends. "They put one of these pointed missiles in the tube, put the tube to their mouth, and blow into it. The missile comes swiftly shooting out. I saw a man shot with one. He was a soldier, a mercenary I had hired to protect us on our journey into the Wild Lands. He died instantly, Tarbizon! The missiles are poisoned in some way." He eyed the other two men. "Imagine many thousands of these creatures armed with such weapons, swarming through the streets of your city and shooting every human they see!"

Florn sucked in his breath, making a sharp hissing sound. Tarbizon nodded, his expression grim. "All right, Armindor, I'm convinced these things are as dangerous as you say they are. Obviously, the question is, What can we do about them?"

"We must figure out how best to fight them, and make plans and preparations," said Armindor. "When I say 'we' I mean all of humanity. Everyone must know of this, Brother, for everyone is going to be involved!"

He swung away from the table and began to pace about the room. "When the reen had me in their power I expected to be killed, and my only regret was that I wouldn't be able to warn anyone about the creatures and their terrible threat to us. Well, thanks to Rood-emiss-Who-Watches-Over-Sages, and thanks to my plucky apprentice here, I survived—and I swore I would carry news of this danger throughout the land. The reen can wipe us out if we're not ready for them, but if people can be warned, we'll have a chance. So people must be made aware of the danger, at once, and especially people in high places, who can do things. I couldn't talk to any of the nobles of Wemms because they're busy trying to kill one another, but I can start here, with the ruler of Inbal. That's why I came straight to you, Brother Tarbizon; I hoped that the sages of Inbal could arrange an audience for me with the High Chairman of the city. I want to show him the dead reen and the weapons, and tell him of the danger so he can take steps to safeguard the people here."

Tarbizon nodded. "I will see to it that you get to talk to the High Chairman of Inbal, Brother," he promised.

··· 4 ···

Several days passed with no word of the audience with the High Chairman of Inbal, and Armindor began to fret. Autumn was giving way to winter, and there was a strong touch of chill in the air. Winter set in quickly in the far north, and Armindor knew that once it did, much of the Silver Sea could quickly become so encrusted with ice that navigation would be impossible, and any ships in the port of Inbal would stay there until the spring thaw set the water free again. Many of the merchant vessels that had been in the harbor had already left on their last voyage before Winterset, and Armindor was aware that if he did not make arrangements to leave on one of the remaining ships soon, it would be too late and he and the others would be forced to spend the winter here in Inbal, which would be a serious blow to his plans. So he fretted and grumbled about the lack of consideration of the High Chairmen, Lord Directors, Lord Speakers, and other nobles who ruled lands and cities. To help pass the time, he and the children went for walks around the city and visited some of its sights, such as the huge wooden statue of the northern hero Diormuk, which had been carved over a century before by a famous artist and which now stood at one end of Inbal's Market Square. On one of these excursions, Armindor bought each of the children a little souvenir gift—a comb made of the pearly, pliable fin of some sea creature, for Jilla; and for Tigg, a small stone-bladed knife with a wood and leather handle.

Finally, after ten days had passed, Tarbizon sent word that the High Chairman had agreed to see Armindor the next day, at the end of the morning session of the High Council of Inbal. The message instructed Armindor to come to the guildhall with Tigg in the morning, pick up the reen exhibits which had been left there, and go to the chairman's palace with Tarbizon, who would introduce them to the chairman and his councilors and vouch for the truth of their story.

After the morning meal, Tigg and Armindor departed, leaving Jilla and Reepah to each other's company. By now, Jilla had grown so used to the grubber's abilities that she regarded him as almost human, but because of his size she tended to think of him as a child rather than the adult he actually was. Thus, she treated him much the same as she treated Tigg, rather than as she did Armindor or any other grown person.

"Do you want to play a game, Reepah?" she asked.

"What is 'kame'?"

"It's—um—something you do for fun. To pass the time," she explained. She taught him the game of Palm, Fist, and Fingers, which she felt he was well able to play with his humanlike hands. This was a game in which each player made either a closed fist or an open hand, or extended three fingers, doing this behind his or her back so that the opponent couldn't see, then revealing the selection simultaneously on the count of three. Three fingers beat an open hand, an open hand beat a fist, and a fist beat three fingers. Jilla and Reepah had nothing to use for prizes, so they simply kept track of wins and losses, with the agreement that the first to have twenty wins would be declared the great winner.

"Is Armindor really going to try to tell every ruler of every land and city about the reen?" asked Jilla, having heard the magician talk of this to Tarbizon. Behind her back she formed a fist.

"He try," said Reepah, his own hand behind his back. "The lands of hyoo-mens must learn of reen before is too late, Jilla. If reen take the world, will be a bitter drink for all living things! The reen are evil. My people, the weenitok, have long fought them. They often attack our communities, to take us as food or as—I not know word, but it means ones who are forced to work hard and treated harshly."

"Slaves," said Jilla soberly.

"Slaves," repeated Reepah. He counted three and displayed an open hand to her closed fist, beating her. "They would do that to some of your people, too, I think. But most they would kill. You are threat to them, and they want you all out of way."

Jilla shivered. "Are there really a lot of them right here in Inbal?"

"Oh, yes. They have strong, ukly smell that fills whole city." His lip curled back in disgust. "None close by, though," he assured her.

She stared at him a bit enviously. Tigg had told her that the grubber had an incredible sense of smell; he had once located Tigg by smell alone in an encampment full of hundreds of other humans, and he had tracked Armindor through the Wild Lands when he and Tigg had become separated from the magician. What would it be like to have such a marvelous ability? wondered the girl.

They whiled away the morning with conversation and sporadic bouts of Palm, Fist, and Fingers, most of which Reepah won, and it was nearing noon when the door of the guestinghouse room was thrust open and Armindor strode in, followed by Tigg. Jilla had never seen the magician angry, and had pretty well decided that he probably never got angry, but she could see that he was certainly angry now. "What's happened?" she gasped.

"They're fools!" exclaimed Armindor. "Fools!" He snatched up a stool, stalked to the room's single window and thrust open the shutters. Putting the stool down with a thud, he sat, staring out of the window with eyes that were obviously focused on his thoughts and not on the view outside.

Tigg plopped down cross-legged by Jilla and the grubber. He sighed. "Everything seemed fine, at first. High Master Tarbizon told them who Armindor was, and how important a sage he is, and of the important spells we'd found in the Wild Lands. Then he told them that Armindor had learned of a dreadful danger and had come to tell them about it, so they could protect the city. They all sat up straight, and looked concerned and interested. Armindor showed the dead reen and the reen weapons, and told them what the reen intended to do. He warned them that there are many reen right here in Inbal, and urged them to begin trying to rid the city of the things. The High Chairman and most of the councilors were all goggle-eyed by now, and looked as if they were ready to go right out and start hunting for reen!

"But then, when Armindor finished talking, one of the councilors stood up and started to talk—a councilor named Leayzar." Tigg's forehead crinkled in a frown, and his dark eyes narrowed with anger. "He all but called Armindor and me liars and tricksters! He said it was nonsense that any such creatures as reen were living in Inbal; no one had ever seen anything like them in the two hundred years since Inbal began!" The boy hopped to his feet and, putting one hand on his hip, he affected a posturing pose. "I have certainly never seen such a creature," he said in a raspy voice with a pronounced northern accent, and Jilla realized he was doing an imitation of the councilor. "Have you? Do you know anyone who has? Of course not—because they don't exist!"

"Bah!" Tigg relaxed his pose and became his scowling self again. "He said the reen body was either some Wild Lands creature or else was just a big rat that we had fixed up to look as it did. He said *we* had made the weapons. He said it was all just a fake that we had worked out with High Master Tarbizon!"

"But why?" asked Jilla. "Why did he think you would do such a thing?"

"For power, he said! He said that the Inbal sages want more power!" Tigg told her. "He shook his finger at High Master Tarbizon and said, 'You wish to make the people of Inbal afraid, so that they will run to you for help. You want them to believe that only you sages can save them!' And then he cried out that he didn't care if the Inbal sages showered him with curses, he was going to speak as he believed, and he was going to advise the High Chairman to ignore the whole 'wild tale'!"

"What happened then?"

Tigg shrugged. "High Master Tarbizon tried to tell the chairman that what Leayzar had said wasn't true, but you could see that the High Chairman didn't believe him. The chairman and all the other councilors had gone over to Leayzar's side. He'd picked them all up and stuffed them into his belt pouch! The High Chairman just thanked Armindor and High Master Tarbizon for their warning, and said he would carefully consider everything they had said, but you could tell that he just wanted us all to go away. So we did."

"But then, they aren't going to do anything about the reen?" asked Jilla in astonishment.

Tigg shook his head. "It doesn't look like it." He scowled. "Well, whatever happens to Inbal will be its own fault!"

Armindor sighed and turned from the window. "Don't judge all of Inbal so harshly, Tigg," he remonstrated gently. "It's not the common people's fault that their rulers often do foolish things. It is the common people of the city who may suffer because of Councilor Leayzar's stupidity." He sighed again. "Well, we've done all we can do here. Perhaps Tarbizon will be able to convince them of the danger in time, but there's nothing more we can do. So I think we had best go down to the docks and see about getting a ship for home as soon as possible."

He looked directly at Jilla. "Jilla, I know you have probably been anxious to be off following your profession as a puppeteer, and I want you to know that Tigg and I are very grateful that you stayed with us for as long as you have. But we've been wondering if we couldn't persuade you to stay and help us out a bit longer—until we get back home to Ingarron. I think you'd like it there, and you could follow your profession there as well as here—Ingarronians love puppet shows too, I assure you. Tigg and I—and Reepah also, I'm sure—would be most happy if you'd come across the Silver Sea with us. Will you?"

Jilla was overwhelmed. She understood fully that Armindor was actually offering to continue looking after her; his remarks about her "profession" were just his way of trying to overcome any reluctance she might have at accepting his charity, and of helping her preserve the fiction that she could survive on her own as a puppeteer—which Jilla had come to realize *was* just a dream. But the fact was, she was looking at Armindor and Tigg in a different way than she had at first. She had now been with them for nearly a moon, and she had become very fond of the kindly, wise man and the cheerful, exuberant boy, and had begun to feel toward them much as she had felt toward Hemm, Ola, and Anjin. She had again come to feel as if she *belonged*. She had known, of course, that they would eventually leave Inbal to return to their home, and she had expected to miss them terribly, but she had not let herself dream of going with them. Armindor's unexpected offer was more than she could have hoped for, and there was only one answer. "Oh, yes," she said, in a voice that was little more than a whisper. Tigg was smiling at her.

"Good!" said Armindor. "Let's be off, then."

They trooped through the door. Jilla was gloriously happy, happier than she had ever thought she could be after her terrible loss in Wemms. Reepah had elected to perch on her shoulder, Tigg was cheerful again, and Armindor, too, had apparently cast off his anger and dismay over the failure to make the rulers of Inbal take heed of his warnings about the reen. Everything seemed wonderful.

But at the docks they ran into bad news. Most of the few ships still in the harbor had been pulled up onto the beach and lay in a long line on the sand, their single, big, triangle-shaped sails removed and their masts forming a row of tall thin fingers pointing toward the sky. Armindor caught sight of some men moving about on one of the ships still in the water, and hailed them, asking about passage across the Silver Sea. He was answered by headshakes. "There'll be no more vessels putting out again until springtime, Your Wisdom," said one of the men. He pointed toward the northern part of the sky, which was dark and filling with heavy gray clouds. "Snow's only a sunrise or two away, and there'll be ice on the water soon after."

"I was afraid of this," said Armindor glumly, turning away. "The Curse of Roodemiss on that scurvy High Chairman for making us wait so long for an audience with him! Trapped in the north during a northern winter! I'll have to buy us all some warm cloaks and foot-wrappings." He sighed. "At least we'll have time to work at figuring out some of those spells and to try getting that box open—but I hate to lose the time that should be spent telling the people of Ingarron, and Orrello, and other places of the reen danger!"

In lower spirits than when they had set out, they made their way back to the Guestinghouse of the North Star. But there, still another unpleasant surprise confronted them. As they entered their room, they uttered exclamations of dismay. The room was a shambles. All their bags of belongings had been opened up and the contents strewn about the floor. The sleeping mats were piled atop one another as if someone had turned them all over to look underneath them.

"There is smell of strange hyoo-men here," announced Reepah.

"We've been robbed!" exclaimed Armindor. "Teeth of Roodemiss, wait till I see the cursed guestinghouse keeper! This shouldn't happen in a decent sort of place!"

Angrily, they began picking up the spare smocks, leg-wrappings, Jilla's puppets, and other things scattered about. After a time, Armindor was frowning in puzzlement.

"Nothing seems to be missing," he said. "It's very strange that a thief would break in and then not take anything at all."

"Yes it is," said Tigg, who knew a great deal about the ways of thieves, having once been one. "There are a lot of things here that he could have got a good price on at a thieves' market."

Armindor looked thoughtful. "It almost seems as if he was looking for something in particular, which he couldn't find, so he left without taking anything. Very odd, although I suppose we should be grateful that we still have all our things." He sighed, shaking his head. "This has been a very trying day. First, the rulers of Inbal refuse to heed our warnings about the reen; then we find we're stuck here for the winter; and now this. I certainly hope tomorrow will turn out better!"

··· 5 ···

The next morning Armindor announced his intention of renting part of a small house in which to spend their winter in Inbal. It would be much too costly, he explained, to continue living and eating in the guesting-house until spring arrived. Not only would the rent of rooms in a house be less than the cost of the guesting-house room, but they could also save money by doing their own marketing and cooking. Tigg and Jilla thought this a charming prospect. And so, following their morning meal, and with a strongly worded demand to the guestinghouse keeper to see to it that their room was kept secure, the magician and his young companions, with Reepah on Jilla's shoulder, started in search of a small, inexpensive, and cozy dwelling that could be their home during the winter months.

It was a cold, gloomy day, and the streets were filled with people who seemed intent on taking care of the last bits of business before winter's first snow began to descend from the dark sky overhead. The sage and the two youngsters wended their way in and out among porters laden with bags and bundles, wealthy merchants in traveling couches borne on the shoulders of sturdy servants, and hornbeast-drawn carts piled with dried vegetables and other provisions. And, turning a corner, the three suddenly found themselves confronted by a crowd of the people known as Mockers.

Mockers were followers of a god named Ornaze, who taught that in order to avoid pain and sorrow, one had to make fun of all aspects of life. On certain days, the members of the Mocker sect in each community would daub their faces with red and green paint, bedeck themselves with fluttering ribbons, and go prancing and cavorting through the streets in observance of their beliefs. Obviously, this was one of those days, and Armindor, Tigg and Jilla became the center of a swirling crowd of noisy, gyrating, painted people.

"A sage, a sage!" yelled one who carried a beribboned stick with an inflated pig bladder tied to one end of it. He bounced this against Armindor's midriff. "Wisdom is nonsense, Sage. It won't ever fill a hungry belly!"

"It won't even fill an empty head," stated another, a woman who thrust her grinning face within inches of Armindor's eyes. "Knowledge is nothing but thoughts, and thoughts themselves are nothing, for they have no substance." She stuck out her tongue. "So your head's full of nothing, Your Wisdom!"

The other Mockers shrieked with laughter at her words and one blew a shrill blast on a curved horn. Armindor stood motionless, keeping his face impassive; Mockers would never do violence to anyone, but if you were foolish enough to show anger or to answer their jibes and jeers, they might make you the focus of their attention for a good long time. The sage knew that if he simply kept silent and still, they would eventually leave him alone.

Fearing that Reepah might be knocked down by the jostling people, Jilla reached up and lifted him off her shoulder, clutching him to her chest and hunching herself forward protectively. The Mocker with the pig bladder bent toward her. "What's that you have, girl, a pet? It's just a useless mouth to feed. You'd do better to cook it and eat it than keep it and feed it!" Jilla, also wise in the ways of these people, said nothing.

Tigg found himself being pushed away from Armindor and Jilla by the jerking, hopping bodies. He let himself move with the pressure rather then struggle and thus draw their attention to him. He thought about how easy it would be to pick a few of the pockets of these foolish people.

The Mockers kept up their jests and noise for a while more, then suddenly they went streaming off in another direction. Armindor heaved a deep and somewhat pained sigh, but made no comment. He glanced around and saw Jilla nearby, then looked for Tigg. He did not see the boy.

"Tigg?" The magician turned slowly in a circle, scanning the street. Tigg was nowhere to be seen.

"Where could he be?" wondered Jilla in a puzzled voice. The crowd had thinned out for a moment, and the end of the street where they were standing was nearly deserted. Unless Tigg had entered one of the shops or dwellings on either side of the street, he had simply vanished from the street completely.

"I don't know," said Armindor slowly. "I do not think he—"

"Are you looking for a certain boy, Your Wisdom?" a wheezing voice interrupted.

Armindor and Jilla turned. An elderly, ragged beggar was sitting cross-legged with his back against the log wall of a house a dozen paces away. He grinned at them out of a heavily bewhiskered face—a grin that showed a great deal of pink gum and only a few scattered yellow teeth. "I can tell you what became of the boy—for a price."

Armindor strode toward him. "What price?" he demanded.

"Oh, just a copper for a couple of meals and a pot or two of beer, Your Wisdom," wheezed the man. It was a large sum, but Armindor quickly dug a copper coin out of his belt pouch and slapped it into the beggar's outstretched hand. "Talk," he grunted.

The beggar became all business, like a merchant taking an order. "When you came onto this street, Your Wisdom, two men carrying a big closed traveling couch came right after you. When the Mockers crowded around you, the men moved off to one side and stopped. The Mockers pushed the boy toward them, and the side of the couch opened up and a man hopped out. He grabbed the boy, hauled him into the couch, and closed it up again. Then the two carriers ran off down the street, that way." He pointed. "They had it all planned, I'd say."

The street curved sharply a few dozen paces away, so even if the men who had abducted Tigg were still on it, they would be hidden from sight. "There's no way to tell where they've gone," said Jilla in dismay. "How can we find him?"

"I can follow his smell," said Reepah.

"Of course!" Armindor exclaimed. "I had forgotten all about that marvelous sense of smell of yours. Thank you, Roodemiss! Show us where to go, Reepah."

"That way," commanded the grubber from Jilla's shoulder, pointing in the direction the beggar had indicated. They set off down the street as fast as the elderly magician could trot, quickly finding themselves once again moving in and out among other people.

"It was all set up, then," growled Armindor. "They must have been following us and were just awaiting their chance, which the Roodemiss-cursed crowd of Mockers provided them! But why do they *want* Tigg?"

"Slavers?" quavered Jilla, horror in her voice. Hemm and Ola had often warned her to beware of the men who abducted children and young men and women to sell into slavery.

"Maybe," said the magician. "But slavers generally don't go to as much trouble as these abductors did. I feel there's something more behind this, but I don't know what."

"Turn here," ordered Reepah when they came to a narrow alley that wound away at one side of the street. Here there were far fewer people, but the way was more constricted and Armindor and Jilla had to squeeze past those they encountered. The alley entered into another street, and here Reepah instructed them to turn left into it. They followed the street past several intersections of other streets, then turned down another winding alley. This brought them to the edge of a small closed square, one side of which was formed by a house of worship, and the other three by rows of small, dilapidated houses. There was a covered well in the exact center of the square.

"Tick in there," stated Reepah, indicating one of the houses directly across from the house of worship.

Armindor considered the house, frowning. "Doesn't look like the sort of place slavers would use," he observed. "No; I don't know what's behind this but, by Roodemiss, now I'm going to find out!"

"Are we going to go get help?" asked Jilla.

The magician shook his head. "There's no time. I don't know what they want Tigg for, but I don't dare leave him in their hands any longer. I'll have to try to get him out of there myself."

"Can you?" worried Jilla, staring at him with wide eyes. "What if there are a lot of them?" It seemed to her that Armindor would be taking a dreadful chance.

"Don't worry," he reassured her. "Even the most vicious thieves and robbers are generally afraid of a magician, and I'll threaten whoever is in there with the most horrible curses they've ever heard! They'll be impressed enough that I've found them; they'll think I have great power." He paused. "That gives me an idea."

He reached into a pocket within his robe and brought forth the little round box with the jiggling pointer that he and Tigg had brought back from the Wild Lands. He was fascinated by this unknown spell, and had kept it, and the Spell of Far-seeing, while he had left the others and the sealed box at the guildhall. Now he held the box steady, waiting for the quivering pointer to come to a stop. When it did, he let out a hiss of delight. "Thanks be to Roodemiss it's pointing almost exactly at the house. What a bit of good luck! This will be the touch of magic that will really put the fear of my power into their hearts!"

He turned to Jilla. "Now listen, Little Maid; you stay right here with Reepah. Keep out of sight and wait." He glanced upward at the sun, a pale, nearly invisible circle in the gloomy sky. "The sun is just about a finger-width away from being right above the tower of that worship house. If I haven't come back with Tigg by the time it's directly above the tower, run to the Sages' Guild-hall and get help. Reepah will find the way back here. Right?"

Jilla nodded. "Garmood and Roodemiss be with you, Armindor."

He smiled at the worried expression on her face, and patted her cheek. Then he turned and strode across the square toward the house where Tigg was being held prisoner by unknown people for an unknown reason.

· · · 6 · · ·

Tigg was seriously considering whether to lift the moneybag of a particularly obnoxious fat and sweating Mocker who kept jostling him, when the boy became aware that he stood beside a big, closed traveling couch held on the shoulders of two burly men who seemed to be regarding him with extreme interest. The traveling couch was a rectangular box, made of pine planks, long and spacious enough for a person to recline, half-sitting, within it. The interior, Tigg knew, was softly upholstered, with raised padding at one end for the occupant's head and shoulders to rest against. Several thin horizontal slits were cut into each side where the occupant's head would be, to let in air and permit the rider to see out. Tigg saw the gleam of eyes peering at him through the side of the couch that faced him. He had only a moment to reflect that both the couch's carriers and its unknown occupant were giving him an undue amount of attention, when suddenly the entire side of the couch flopped down, revealing itself to be hinged at the bottom, and a man launched himself out of the interior, landing on the balls of his feet behind Tigg, so close that the startled boy could feel the warmth of his body. A rough hand clamped itself over Tigg's mouth, an arm encircled his chest, crushing his arms flat against his sides, and he was swung upward and stuffed into the couch, shoved flat against its far side. An instant later the man had followed him in and was pressing against him. The open side of the couch was slammed shut, and Tigg felt the conveyance lurch into swift motion.

Something cold and sharp touched his chin. "One sound out of you, boy," a brutal voice said into his ear, "and I'll slice your throat open!"

Tigg's reaction, as was usual when someone committed what he felt to be an injustice against him, was anger, and he instantly vowed vengeance on this person who was threatening him. But in his street-running days as a thief in Ingarron he had learned that it was easier to get even with an enemy if that enemy thought he was harmless. Nothing was more harmless than a frightened child, so Tigg drew on his considerable ability as an actor.

"Please don't hurt me!" he whimpered.

The pressure of the knife on his chin grew less as the man relaxed, and Tigg smiled to himself. "Just do as you're told and you won't get hurt," the man growled.

Tigg considered the words and the man's reaction. He felt that the fellow was probably trying to keep him in a state of fear, but was also trying to reassure him somewhat so that he wouldn't be overwhelmed with terror and possibly become hysterical. This decided Tigg that he hadn't been taken by slavers, because he was well aware, from having seen slavers operate in the streets of Ingarron, that their usual method of keeping a child under control was simply to batter it into unconsciousness. So these presumably weren't slavers, but then who were they, and what in Garmood's name did they want with *him*?

The boy was not particularly frightened, because he knew that Reepah's marvelous sense of smell would be able to locate him wherever in Inbal his captors might take him, and he was confident that Armindor would soon come to rescue him. But he was intensely curious as to why these men would have gone to so much trouble to seize a common, ordinary-looking boy. He wondered if perhaps they had mistaken him for someone else.

Nevertheless, he intended to do everything he could to get even with them for interfering with his liberty, subjecting him to mauling, and squashing his nose against the musty-smelling upholstery of the couch's side. He concentrated on trying to figure out their route; he knew they had started up the same street on which they had seized him, and now he felt the couch swing sharply to the right as the bearers apparently turned into another street. Tigg filed that in his memory and kept careful track of every other turn they made. He wanted to learn how to get to wherever they were taking him, so that he could come back some time after he escaped from them and wreak his vengeance!

Abruptly, the bearers stopped. "Hold still," commanded the man in the couch with him, and passed a folded strip of cloth over his eyes and around his head, knotting it tightly at the back of his skull. Interesting, thought Tigg; they don't want me to see where I am. That meant they were probably going to let him go eventually, because if they intended to keep him, or even kill him, they wouldn't have cared if he knew where he was.

He heard sounds that told him the side of the couch had been let down, and moments later the pressure of the man's body against him was removed. Then he was hauled out of the compartment, set on his feet, given a slight nudge to start him walking, and guided along by the pressure of a heavy hand on his shoulder.

His first steps told him he was walking on the packed dirt of a city street, then a difference in the feeling of the substance beneath his feet indicated that he had gone into some kind of building. He was guided along for a dozen or so paces, then he heard a door squeak slightly in front of him.

"Downstairs," grunted the voice of the man who had been in the couch with him. "Ten steps."

With the man's hand still on his shoulder, Tigg carefully descended. A slight feeling of dampness and chilliness, and a faint musty scent that came creeping into his nostrils, led him to believe he must be in a cellar.

"Sit," said the man.

Tigg cautiously lowered himself until he touched a flat, cool surface that was surely the seat of a stool. The man pulled his arms back and proceeded to tie his wrists together. Obviously, his captors didn't want him removing his blindfold. He heard the sound of footsteps *shuff-shuff-shuffing* up the stairs, then heard the door thump shut.

He cocked his head and listened, holding his breath. After several moments he had not heard the slightest sound, so he concluded he was alone. He tested his bonds. They were tight, but he felt sure he would work his way out of them in time. He began to twist and wriggle his arms, ignoring the pain as the leather rope bit into his skin. If he could free himself, he might be able to escape unseen. He felt sure he was in an ordinary small house; if he could get through the cellar door he could make a dash for the door that led to the outside. The knife that Armindor had given him as a present was wrapped in the twisted cloth that served him as a belt and, if necessary, he would have no compunctions about planting it in someone's belly if they tried to stop him!

Quite close to him a voice whispered, "Boy."

Tigg gave a guilty jump and stopped his efforts to slip out of his bonds. Had someone been in here with him all along then, watching? He could have sworn he was alone. "Who's there?" he asked.

"That does not matter," replied the whispered voice. There was an odd quality to it that the boy could not place. He felt that the whisperer might be trying to disguise his or her voice. "I shall ask you some questions and you will answer," the whisper continued. "You were in the place called the Wild Lands with the man known as Armindor the Magician. There, you and he found some ancient objects from the Age of Magic, which you brought here to this city. Where are they now?"

Tigg was rather surprised by such a question. He felt sure that by now a great many people must know about the spells he and Armindor had found in the Wild Lands; probably every sage in Inbal now knew of them, and Armindor had also spoken of them before the entire council of the city, and surely many of these people must have told friends and members of their families. But Tigg was surprised that his questioner didn't know, or hadn't guessed, that Armindor had simply left most of the spells at the Sages' Guildhall for safekeeping. Well, if this person didn't know that, Tigg certainly wasn't going to enlighten him.

"I don't know, Great One," he squeaked, slipping back into his frightened-little-boy act. "Soon after we arrived here, Armindor took everything off somewhere by himself. He said that he had hidden it all, but he did not tell me where."

There was a pause, as if the person was thinking this over. Then the whispered voice said, "Will he be willing to give up the objects to get you back?"

So that's why they stole me, thought Tigg. All this because of the spells. But who *are* they? What does this person want magic for? "Oh, I'm sure he would, Great One," the boy babbled. If they thought he could be useful to them, they were more likely to give him good treatment. Meanwhile, he'd try to find out as much as he could. "But why do you want them, Great One? Are you a magician?"

"That is of no matter to you," said the whisperer. "It is—" It broke off suddenly, and in the complete silence Tigg became aware of the muffled sound of a raised voice coming from somewhere overhead. As he listened, it seemed to grow louder and nearer. There was an angry-sounding hiss from the direction of the whisperer, followed by a rustling noise and then a faint thump. Moments later, Tigg heard the sound of the door at the top of the stairs creaking open.

"Tigg?" called the anxious voice of Armindor. "Are you all right?"

··· 7 ···

Standing before the house in which Tigg was being held
prisoner, Armindor banged loudly on the door with the
heel of his fist. He did not have to wait long before the
door was jerked open and he was confronted by a thin,
middle-size man with pale eyes and a frizzy burst of
yellow hair, whose angry scowl indicated his annoyance
at having to answer the magician's knock. But at the
sight of Armindor the scowl vanished as the man's eyes
opened wide and his jaw dropped in surprise. Obviously he recognized the sage, and this told Armindor that
the fellow must have been watching him, Tigg, and
Jilla for some time.

"Yes, you know me, I think," rumbled the magician.
"And I know you! Fool, did you think you could steal
something from a *magician* and get away with it? Why,
my magic has led me straight to you!" Armindor wanted
to impress the man with his "power"; it might make
things easier.

The man *was* impressed. He had never even expected

to see the magician, and to be suddenly confronted by
Armindor less than half a morning after his apprentice
had been seized, indicated tremendous power. Like most
people, he had a healthy fear of sages, and now he
mentally cursed the greed that had made him take part
in the plot to steal the magician's apprentice.

Desperately, he tried to bluff his way out of the situation. "I don't know what you mean, Your Wisdom. I
swear I never stole anything of yours," He began to
nudge the door shut.

Armindor thrust out an arm, pushing the door back
open with such force that the man involuntarily took a
step backward. The magician stepped into the doorway.
He was nearly a head taller than the kidnapper, and his
big body almost filled the door frame. He had often
used his imposing size to dominate others, and he used
it now to add to the man's obvious fear of him. "Do not
try to lie," he snarled. "You seized my apprentice and
carried him here in a traveling couch. I want him back!"

The fact that Armindor even knew how the kidnapping had been carried out added to the man's dismay,
but he tried one more time to put Armindor off the
track. "It wasn't me, Your Wisdom! You've got the wrong
man!"

Armindor stuck a hand in his robe and brought out
the round box with the quivery pointer, thrusting it
under the man's nose. "See this?" he roared. "It is a Spell
of Truth-finding. Watch that thin shiny thing that is
spinning around. If it stops moving and points into this
house, it will prove that you lie!"

The man stared at the box as if it were a venomous
snake rearing to strike at him. He had, of course, never
seen anything remotely like it. The shiny texture of the

plastic box had a shockingly alien look to a person familiar only with wood, stone, cloth, and leather, while the quivering, jittering, shimmering needle seemed like an uncanny living thing. To be confronted by this example of the tremendous forces at Armindor's command was the last blow for the kidnapper, and when the compass needle finally quivered to a stop, pointing straight at him (to Armindor's concealed delight), a moan of fear oozed between his lips.

Armindor pushed his way into the house, the man giving way weakly before him. The magician now felt sure that he had only this one man to deal with; if there had been others in the house they would have shown up by now. "All right, then," he said, putting the compass back into his robe. "You take me to the boy now, or in the name of Roodemiss, the Spirit of the Magic of Earth, Air, Fire, and Water, I'll lay a curse on you that will shrivel the flesh off your bones—slowly!"

The man wilted completely. "Have mercy, Your Wisdom! I'm not the one responsible for this. I was just doing a job, and believe me, I'm sorry as a deadwalker's dinner that I agreed to do it! He hired me to steal the boy from you and bring him here."

"Who hired you?" questioned Armindor.

"Pan Biblo—Councilor Leayzar's top servant."

Armindor managed to keep his face impassive, but he was severely startled. Councilor Leayzar was, of course, the member of the Inbal High Council who had accused him and the magicians of Inbal of lying about the danger from the reen and had convinced the High Chairman to pay no attention to Armindor's warnings, and Armindor could not imagine why he would be involved in Tigg's abduction. For the magician felt sure the servant of so important a man would never have acted on his own; this Pan Biblo must have had Tigg kidnapped on orders from Leayzar. But why would a nobleman of a great city go to so much trouble to steal a common little apprentice magician?

"Take me to the boy," he ordered.

The man scurried a few steps along a short hallway and opened a door. "He's down here, Your Wisdom."

"Tigg?" called Armindor anxiously. "Are you all right?"

"I'm fine," came Tigg's voice from the cellar. He gave a little giggle. "It sure didn't take you long to find me!"

There was a candle burning in a clay holder in a wall niche by the door, and Armindor picked it up. "Lead the way," he told the kidnapper, gesturing at the door, "and no tricks or you'll deeply regret it!"

They passed down the stone stairs into a small stone-walled cellar occupied only by a square wooden table and two stools, on one of which was perched Tigg, his hands tied behind his back and a piece of cloth wrapped around his eyes. "Untie him," Armindor ordered, and he slid the cloth up off Tigg's head, tousling the boy's hair into an untidy thatch.

Tigg blinked and peered about, "Why, where could he have gone?" he said in a puzzled voice.

"Who?"

"There was someone here talking to me," explained Tigg, frowning as he leaned forward to stare into corners left in deep shadows by the single candlelight. "He was asking questions and then you came. But I don't see any way out of here except for the door at the top of the stairs."

"Who was down here with the boy?" Armindor demanded of the kidnapper, who had finished untying

Tigg and now stood nervously wringing his hands.

"I don't know, Your Wisdom," said the man earnestly. "Biblo told me just to put the boy into the cellar and leave him alone, blindfolded and tied. He said he'd tell me what was to be done with him later."

"Is there a hidden entrance to this cellar?" asked Armindor.

The man shrugged. "I don't know, Your Wisdom, I don't live here. Biblo told me to bring the boy here and wait, and that's what I did. I don't know anything about the place."

"Well, you can be sure there's a secret way in and out of here, Tigg," Armindor assured the boy, looking about. "People don't just vanish out of places. What was this person questioning you about?"

"He wanted to know where the spells we brought back from the Wild Lands are," said Tigg, looking at Armindor with a serious expression. "I told him I didn't know. He asked if I thought you would be willing to trade the spells to get me back."

"So that's what this was all about!" exclaimed Armindor. "Councilor Leayzar wants the ancient magic and had you stolen because he thought you could tell him where it is." He clapped his hand in a gesture of sudden understanding. "And that's why our room at the guestinghouse was burgled last night—they were looking for the spells!"

"Councilor Leayzar?" said Tigg in surprise. "But what would *he* want with spells of magic?"

Armindor shook his head. "I have no idea. A common thief might want them to sell, a renegade magician might want them just to own, but what could a wealthy nobleman with no training in magic want them for?" He looked thoughtfully at Tigg. "You have heard Leayzar's voice—was it he who questioned you?"

"I don't know," Tigg told him regretfully. "Whoever it was was whispering and disguising his voice. He sounded strange."

"Well, Leayzar is playing some kind of deep game; that is clear," said the magician. "I had better tell Tarbizon of this as soon as possible, and see what he thinks." He turned to look sharply at the kidnapper, who stood in a cringing posture behind Tigg. "Tell your employer, Biblo, how easily my powers enabled me to spoil his master's plan, and tell him that Leayzar would be wise to forget all about trying to get hold of those spells!" He hoped that this man might tell such a tale of powerful magic that the councilor would decide to give up any further schemes.

But the kidnapper shook his head vigorously. "I don't dare ever see Pan Biblo or any other of Councilor Leayzar's men, Your Wisdom. They'd tie logs to my legs and sink me in the harbor for letting you come in here and take this boy! I'm leaving Inbal this very day. I'll go to Wemms; it'll be safer for me there, war or no war." He glanced anxiously around the cellar. "And we'd better all get out of here, Your Wisdom, before whoever was down here with the boy comes back with help!"

"I suspect you're right," the magician agreed. "Come on, Tigg."

They were no sooner all out of the front door of the house than the kidnapper took to his heels. Tigg watched him go, frowning. "I hate to see him get away. He should be punished!"

"He's being punished," Armindor assured the boy. "A winter in Wemms in the middle of a war is a grim prospect!" He glanced up at the tower of the house of worship across the square. "Good; it didn't take long to get you out of there. I was hoping I could do it before Jilla and Reepah had to go to the guildhall for help."

Jilla had seen them come out of the house, and now she darted out of her hiding place and came flying toward them, Reepah clutching tightly to her head. "You're safe!" she exclaimed, giving Tigg a powerful hug—to his embarrassment. Reepah was happily squeaking, "Tick! Tick!"

Jilla then hugged Armindor. "You did it!" she exclaimed. "I was afraid something would go wrong."

"It was a little easier than I thought it would be," Armindor confessed. He looked back at the shabby house, its door still standing ajar. "Let's be away from here before any of Leayzar's servants show up and try to stop us. They might not be as easily impressed as that other fellow was."

They hurried out of the square into the narrow alley. "But what happened?" questioned Jilla. "Who were they and why did they take Tigg?"

"It was all the work of none other than Councilor Leayzar, the man who made the High Chairman of Inbal refuse to pay any attention to my warning about the reen," Armindor told her. "For some reason he wants the spells Tigg and I brought out of the Wild Lands. He doesn't know that I left them at the guildhall, except for the two I carry with me, and he had our room searched yesterday in hope of finding them there. When that didn't work, he had Tigg carried off with the idea of forcing him to tell where they are."

"Did they hurt you, Tigg?" Jilla asked, looking anxiously at the boy.

He shook his head. "No. They blindfolded me and tied me up and put me down in a cellar. Then someone came and asked me questions. He spoke in a whisper and disguised his voice so that it sounded kind of—hissy."

Armindor stopped short. "Hissy?" he said, frowing.

"Yes," said Tigg as he and Jilla stopped also. He looked sharply at the magician, aware that Armindor seemed suddenly concerned. "Does that mean something?"

"It might," said Armindor. "Look, my young friends, I think we must put off our search for a house today. Too much has happened. I don't think Leayzar will give up trying to get hold of the ancient magic, and I must get to the guildhall and warn Tarbizon and the others to be doubly on guard. And I feel I should get that sealed box open immediately and find out what's in it." He rubbed his forehead thoughtfully. "It's just possible that Leayzar might try to have our room searched again, and this time he might have his burglar take some of my books of spells or devices of magic. It might be best if the three of you kept an eye on things there while I go to the guildhall. I don't think you'll be in any danger; a burglar wouldn't enter an occupied room, and besides, after the scolding I gave the guestinghouse keeper I think he and his two husky sons will be on guard. I think the guestinghouse is probably the safest place for you." He dipped into his belt pouch. "Here's some money so you can buy a meal. I'll try to rejoin you by sunset."

Tigg and Jilla exchanged quick glances but said nothing. They could both see that Armindor was worried. The three of them, with Reepah still on Jilla's shoulder, made their way along the alley, skirting an occasional pile of garbage, until they came to the street. There they said their good-byes, and the boy and girl turned off to head back to the guestinghouse. Armindor stood and watched them until they were out of sight. Then he peered sharply about in all directions, up and down the narrow dirt street and into the shadowy places between the pale wooden buildings on each side. His face wearing a frown of concern, he turned and strode off in the direction of the Guildhall of the Sages of Inbal.

• • • 8 • • •

Luckily, the head of the sages of Inbal, Armindor's old friend High Master Tarbizon, was again at the guildhall when Armindor got there. He listened soberly to Armindor's account of the kidnapping of Tigg and the discovery that Councilor Leayzar was trying to get hold of the ancient magical objects from the Wild Lands.

"I cannot imagine what he would want with them," he said, furiously stroking his beard. "But it's a bad situation, Brother! He's wealthy enough and powerful enough to cause you more trouble. Be on your guard."

"I shall be," Armindor promised. "But I fear there may even be more to this than meets the eye. Tigg told me of something that has disturbed me greatly. While he was a captive he was blindfolded and put into a cellar where he was questioned by someone who spoke only in a whisper, in what Tigg described as a peculiar hissing voice." He leaned forward, peering through the candlelight into Tarbizon's eyes as if to be sure that what he said was fully understood. "Tarbizon, when I talked with that reen that held me captive in the Wild Lands, it spoke our language perfectly except for a noticeable *hissing* accent. I fear that Tigg was questioned by a reen!"

Tarbizon started. "But that would mean—"

"Yes, it would mean that Leayzar is working with or for the reen," said Armindor, finishing the other's thought. "He wouldn't be the first human to do so, Brother; I've told you of that mercenary soldier who had been bought by gold the reen gave him. But if Leayzar is working for the reen, it would explain a lot of things. It would explain why he attacked our attempts to warn the people of Inbal about the reen, and it would also explain why he's so interested in trying to get hold of the things Tigg and I brought out of the Wild Lands— not for himself, but for *them*! They want those things; that was why some of them followed us to the Wild Lands in the first place, as I told you."

Tarbizon grimaced. "This is sickening, Armindor. How could a man ally himself with creatures that intend to destroy his own kind?"

"They may not have told him of their intentions," said Armindor. "Who knows what they told him, or promised him, or gave him?" He looked about. They were in the place known as the Room of Valuables, where the objects from the Wild Lands were being kept with the treasures of the Inbal Sages' Guild—a large cellar below the building's ground floor, with walls and floor formed of big rough blocks of stone held together with mortar. Massive wooden cabinets stood against the walls, and heavy wooden chests sat on the floor, all sealed with heavy locks of wood and stone, contrived by a people who had no metal to use for such things. "If reen are involved in this, the situation is far more dangerous than we've supposed," said Armindor. "If they or Leayzar find out that what they want is here, they might try to get it, perhaps by breaking through the walls from the other side, or digging up through the floor. You can be sure they have tools, and Roodemiss knows how many of them there may be, hiding in the gutters and cellars and underground tunnels of the city!"

"I don't think you need fear," Tarbizon told him. "These walls and the floor were built especially to keep out rats and mice that might work their way in and chew up valuable books or other treasures, and they are kept in good repair. We check them twice yearly to make sure there are no loose blocks or crumbling mortar. And the door at the head of the stairs is made from a northern stonewood tree and is as thick as the length of my forearm. I don't think anything could break into this place, Brother, but to help make certain I shall put a double guard on it night and day: one man here in the room and one outside the door."

"That will help me sleep easier," acknowledged Armindor. "But I tell you, Brother, I don't think I want to wait any longer to get that sealed box open and see what is in it. If it *should* somehow get stolen before we even know what it contains, I would be doubly distraught!"

Tarbizon nodded. "I understand, Armindor. But let me get some of the other brothers and sisters down here to help and to watch. Opening that box may be a major event in the history of magic!"

Shortly, half-a-dozen other blue-robed men and women sages were in the room, gathered about the stout wooden table on which the mysterious box had been placed. Jilla might have giggled again, to see how they were as excited as little children at festival time

"It looks as if the only thing to do is work at it with hammers and chisels," said one, examining the strip of gray metal that ran around all four sides of the rectangular box.

"I think I would counsel against that, Brother," cautioned another. "Whatever is inside may be very delicate. Hammering might shatter it!"

An elderly woman with flowing hair and shaggy white eyebrows moistened her finger with her tongue and scrubbed at the metal strip. Then she scratched at the metal with her thumbnail and peered closely to see the result. "I believe I know what this stuff is, High Master Armindor," she said excitedly. "I got hold of a fair-size amount of it to experiment with once, many years ago."

"This is Sister Chuveen," Tarbizon introduced the woman to Armindor. "She has long specialized in the study of ancient metals."

"If it is indeed what I think it is, High Master," said Chuveen, looking at Armindor, "the best way to get it off would be with fire. I discovered that it melts rather easily."

"Try it, Sister," said Armindor after a moment.

Chuveen picked up one of the many candles clustered on the table beside the box and tilted it so that the flame washed over a finger-width section of the metal strip. "I once tested bits of many different kinds of metal with fire," she said. "Most of them simply became hot. Some changed color slightly. But there was one that melted into a silvery liquid, and I think this is the same kind as that."

She continued to hold the candle against the metal as minutes passed. Then—"There it goes!" shouted someone. The portion of metal washed by the flame was suddenly flowing down the side of the box in a silvery trickle, revealing the seam that it had been covering.

"All right," said Armindor, his voice thick with joy, "everyone pick up a candle and let's get to work. My honor to your knowledge, Sister Chuveen!"

It took the better part of an hour, but eventually the strip was off and the entire seam running around the box could be seen. The eight blue-robed sages stood staring at the box with expressions ranging from wild elation to apprehensive fear.

"It is your discovery, Brother Armindor," said Tarbizon quietly. "You open it."

Armindor licked his lips and leaned forward, inserting his fingertips into the seam on each of the short sides of the box. "We may have to pry it open with chisels," he remarked. "It seems to be pretty tight. But I'll see if I can—oh!" To his surprise, the top portion of the box lifted up quite easily.

And what happened then, none of the sages could have imagined in their most feverish dreams.

As the lid of the box swung up and back, a thin gray square, half the size of the box, lifted up and stood upright. Beneath it, flush with the rim of the box, was a flat gray surface studded with a row of slightly raised circles, each a different color—red, blue, yellow, green, black, white. A tiny red light glowed like a jewel in sunlight. And from somewhere within the box, to the amazement of the sages, some of whom stepped back in alarm, a voice began to speak in an unknown language.

"Greetings to you from the year twenty-oh-three. This is Doctor Dennis Hammond of the National Science Foundation Project for the Preservation of Civilization. It has become obvious that war between the nations of the Pan-Islamic Brotherhood and the United States and its allies of Europe, Canada, the Soviet Union, and China is imminent. It is also obvious that this will be an all-out thermonuclear war, inasmuch as the fundamentalist leaders of the Pan-Islamic Brotherhood are firmly convinced that they have divine assurance they can use atomic missiles with no danger to themselves. It is the concerted opinion of the majority of those in the physical and biological sciences in the United States and among our allies that a thermonuclear war of the scope expected will result in the destruction of much of the plant and animal life throughout the world, and will produce conditions rendering it impossible for civilization to continue. Therefore, we are activating the plan we have been working on for a number of years, in hope that the basic elements of our scientific knowledge and the history of our planet may be preserved and passed on to the future.

"A quantity of units such as the one you have activated will be put in protected areas throughout North America with the hope that one will eventually be discovered. They consist of a computer, memory storage bank, gel-screen, ceramic ring battery with a life of ten-thousand-plus years—and a number of other parts, the names of which will probably be meaningless to you. But they contain the knowledge of humankind, from the thoughts of Plato to the formula for an electricity-conducting ceramic material. If civilization has been lost, this will enable you to regain it!"

The voice paused for a moment, as the sages listened uncomprehending, in stunned silence. Then it continued.

"It is possible that hundreds of years may pass before any of these units are discovered and activated, and the linguists tell us the language may change drastically during that time and the English I am speaking now may not be understandable. Therefore we have programmed the units to begin with a sequence of language instruction, and when I finish speaking the gel-screen will show a pictogram designed to instruct any viewer who cannot understand me to press the red button. If you can understand me, ignore this and press the blue button; obviously you won't need language lessons."

Again there was a short pause, and then, with a catch in his voice, the speaker said, "We your ancestors wish you good luck, happiness, and peace."

The voice stopped completely. On the gray surface of the upright square there appeared an image of a hand, shown as a black outline, with its forefinger extended and pressing a red circle. When it was apparent that the voice had stopped for good, the sages began to stir out of their frozen astonishment.

"How can this be?" asked one in almost a whisper, staring at the box. "How can this box talk? Can it *think*? Is it then *alive* somehow?"

"Perhaps that was the voice of Roodemiss!" exclaimed another, awe in his tone.

"I think," said Armindor slowly, "that we are participating in the greatest spell of magic that has been seen in this world since the Age of Magic came to an end. I think that what we have just heard was the voice of a magician of the Age of Magic, somehow preserved inside this box!"

"But what did he say?' asked the young sage Florn plaintively. "Why couldn't we understand him?"

"Obviously they spoke a different language in those days," said Tarbizon, fingering his beard. "We have no actual writings from the Age of Magic itself; the oldest books we have were written many hundreds of years later, recording things that were handed down by word of mouth for generations before. As you know, they are in a language much like ours, but even it has many differences and unknown words. Apparently language changed slowly over the centuries."

"But then how will we understand what the voice is saying?" questioned another of the sages.

"I think the box wants us to do something," suggested the old sage Chuveen. "That picture of a hand poking at a red circle—I think it is showing us that we should poke the red circle of that row of circles on the box. Maybe that will help us understand somehow."

"You are right, Sister Chuveen," said Armindor. "I think this spell was made to do far more than just give one speech and show one picture. Very well, I shall press the red circle, if no one objects."

Several of the sages drew back apprehensively, as if fearful of what might happen, but no one said anything. Armindor put his finger on the red button and exerted pressure. Instantly the picture on the gray square vanished. Its place was taken by a scene showing what was obviously a stretch of green grass, a single tree, a distant line of blue mountains over which floated a single cloud, and above all, a bright yellow circle that surely represented the sun. Next to this circle, a black arrow began to blink on and off.

"Sun," said a pleasant female voice. "Sun—sun—sun—sun." The arrow vanished from beside the circle and appeared, blinking, beside the cloud. "Cloud," said the voice. "Cloud—cloud—cloud—cloud."

Tarbizon caught on. "It is teaching us words of the ancient tongue!" he shouted. "Florn, get writing materials down here quickly." The young sage bolted up the stairs.

"Hurry, hurry!" old Chuveen called anxiously after him. She glanced apologetically at Tarbizon and Armindor. "We will lose so much if it isn't written down right away."

"Don't worry," said Armindor almost dreamily. "I'm sure it will be able to tell us thousands of words over and over, so we'll have plenty of time to write them down and become familiar with them. The ancient magicians will have thought of everything, Sister Chuveen." He turned to Tarbizon. His eyes were spilling tears, but he wore a smile that made his face seem to glow "This is it, Brother. This is what every magician has been praying for since the Guild of Sages was formed two hundred years ago. The key to all magic! It is in this box for us, Tarbizon; I know it is! All we have to do is learn the language and press the other colored circles!"

Tarbizon nodded. His face, too, was radiant. "Yes. This is the greatest event in three thousand years, Armindor, and it is your doing. Honor to you!"

Florn came charging down the stairs, almost tripping in his haste, a cluster of charcoal writing sticks in one hand and a bundle of cloth writing squares in the other. He quickly passed one of each out to the five other lesser sages, who bent over the table, listening carefully to the sound of the words spoken by the voice, writing them down in the alphabet of the current language, and writing their meanings alongside them.

Florn then turned to Armindor. "High Master, those two children—your apprentice and the girl—are upstairs. I told them you were doing something very important, but they said they must see you at once. They said to tell you that something has happened that threatens you all with great danger!"

··· 9 ···

"He's worried, isn't he?" asked Jilla, glancing over her shoulder at Armindor as she and Tigg started back toward the guestinghouse. "He thinks this Leayzar is going to cause more trouble."

"Yes," the boy acknowledged. "And he's worried about something else, too. He got upset when I told him that the person who questioned me had a hissing voice. That meant something special to him, but I'm not sure what." He sighed. "I wish he'd tell us, but that's not his way. He doesn't want *us* to be worried. But maybe we could help."

The day had become wintry, and Jilla clutched her cloak more tightly about herself, taking care not to disturb Reepah, who was slumbering on her shoulder. "I guess we should be careful if we're in danger from Leayzar." She made a face. "It isn't fair that he should be able to have our room burgled and have you stolen and get away with it. He should be judged!"

Tigg made a rude noise. "Nobles don't get judged.

Only poor people do. Nobles can do whatever they want."

"That's what Hemm—my foster father—always said, too," murmured Jilla. A big black-and-red merchant wagon drawn by a pair of the huge piglike creatures called squnts was rumbling up the street, and they moved in close to the log wall of a house to let it pass. Jilla yawned. "I'm hungry. Shall we eat in the guestinghouse eating room or shall we look for a street vendor and get some pies or something?"

"Let's do both," suggested the boy with a grin. "I like that spicy catmeat stew they make at the guestinghouse, but I like the seafood you can get in Inbal, too. My city, Ingarron, is far from the sea, and I'd never tasted seafood until I came traveling with Armindor."

Heading back toward the guestinghouse, they kept their eyes open for a vendor of seafood and finally spotted one, sitting cross-legged beside his clay grill full of glowing charcoal and his assortment of freshly caught sea creatures in a pot of water. Tigg settled for three small plump octopuses, grilled on a wooden skewer and coated with vinegary sauce, and Jilla had a skewer of grilled fish chunks. They continued slowly on their way, munching as they went, but the seafood did no more than take the edge off their appetites, and they both felt ready for another meal when they reached the guestinghouse.

The entrance to the guestinghouse led directly into the eating room, but Tigg and Jilla passed through it and went to first check their sleeping room, remembering Armindor's fear that it might be burgled again. Everything was as they had left it that morning, so they turned back down the short corridor that connected to the eating room. But at the eating room entrance, Tigg stopped short and clutched at Jilla to keep her from continuing. The place was full of soldiers—four hard-faced men and three tough-looking women—in leather coats covered with overlapping rectangles of animal horn, and bearing short, stabbing spears with razor-edged points of black volcanic glass. Such soldiers were often employed as a private police force and bodyguard for wealthy nobles, and Tigg's instincts as a former thief and pick-pocket were screaming out a warning that whenever this many soldiers came into a place, it meant trouble for someone.

The leader of the soldiers was a thick-bodied man with red hair tied in a bun at the back of his neck and spiraling blue tattoos on his cheeks, which marked him as a member of one of the northern tribes that wor-shiped a sky god called Thamis. He was talking to the guestinghouse keeper, and luckily he had a loud, boom-ing voice. Tigg and Jilla stood silently in the corridor and took in his words.

"You have a sage by the name of Arimdor or some such thing staying here, right?" questioned the soldier. "A big, baldheaded man with a southern accent, eh?"

"Why, yes, Captain, but he isn't in right now," an-swered the keeper, sounding nervous. "He and the two children he has with him went out this morning and aren't back yet." Fortunately, the keeper was turned away from the corridor entrance and hadn't seen Tigg and Jilla.

"Well, our master, Councilor Leayzar, wants to talk with him and sent us to fetch him," boomed the soldier, "so we'll just wait around until he gets back." He wiped his lips with the back of his hand. "How's your beer, keeper?"

"Quick," whispered Tigg to Jilla. "Our room."

They darted down the corridor and into the room, where Tigg quickly barred the door. "We've got to warn Armindor," the boy said in a low voice. "If he comes back and they take him to Leayzar, we may never see him again! Leayzar wants those spells badly, and I think he'd torture Armindor to death to get them!"

"He wouldn't dare," said Jilla, shocked. "Armindor's a magician. He would put a curse on Leayzar."

"Nobles aren't as afraid of magicians as most other people are," Tigg informed her. He was hurriedly collecting Armindor's books of spells and stuffing them into his smock. "They can afford to hire another magician to remove any curses that might be put on them. That's what Leayzar would do, so he wouldn't care how Armindor might curse him. Come on, Jilla, we won't be able to come back to this room again, so we've got to gather up as many of our things as we can and get out of here."

"But they'll see us," she protested. "We have to go through the eating room to get out."

"No." He jerked his head toward the single shuttered window in the wall that faced onto the street. "We'll go out the window." He scooped up one of the bags of their belongings.

Jilla picked up the bag that contained her puppets and some clothing. Reepah suddenly came awake on her shoulder. "What is happening?" he asked, sounding bewildered.

While Jilla explained, Tigg dragged a stool to the

window and, kneeling on it, he opened the shutters and stuck his head and shoulders through the opening. "Come on, quick," he urged. "There's no one on the street now, but if someone comes along and sees us coming out of this window we could be taken for thieves and that would mean bad trouble." He drew back in, swung himself forward, and slithered feet first through the opening.

Jilla darted to the window and hopped onto the stool. "Hang on tight," she told Reepah. Clutching the bag, she thrust herself feet first through the window as Tigg had done.

From the first-floor window the drop to the ground wasn't much more than the height of a tall man, and Jilla landed lightly on her feet, steadied by Tigg's outstretched hand. "Come on," he said, "the guildhall is this way, I think."

They scurried around the corner, narrowly missing a collision with a stout matron who gave a squawk of surprise as they whizzed past her, and ran the length of the street to the next intersection. There Tigg paused, uncertainly. "I don't remember if we go left or right. Reepah, can you find the way to Armindor?"

There was no answer. Jilla craned her head to look at the grubber, whose handlike paws clutched her cloak on each side of her neck. "He's asleep again," she said in disbelief.

Tigg peered closely at the little creature. "He's been falling asleep more and more lately," he said, concern in his voice. "I hope he's not sick! We have trouble enough!" He glanced anxiously from side to side. "Well— let's go right."

As it turned out, he had chosen the correct way, and

before long they sighted the large building with the blue banner swaying from its front. They hurried into the entrance alcove and Tigg raised himself on tiptoe to yank the braided leather cord that sounded the wooden gong within.

The door was opened by a chubby young sage with a clean-shaven face, who eyed the two children with an air of suspicion. "What do you want?"

"Elder Brother," said Tigg, carefully using the proper form of address from an apprentice to a lesser sage, as Armindor had taught him, "I am the apprentice of High Master Armindor of Ingarron. He came here today to consult with some of the Master Sages. We must see him! Something has happened he must know about!"

The chubby sage's face took on an expression of agonized indecision. He was reluctant to let a couple of children into the building, but equally reluctant to turn them away lest he gain the displeasure of a High Master. The rapid *flap-flap-flap* of sandals coming down the hallway toward him drew his attention, and he stretched out an arm to halt the sage who was hurrying by. "Brother Florn! This boy says he's the apprentice of that Ingarron High Master who's down in the Room of Valuables with High Master Tarbizon. Is it true?"

Florn, clutching his writing stick and squares, skidded to a stop and looked at Tigg. "Yes, it's true. But High Master Armindor is doing something very important now, Apprentice Tigg; I don't think he'll want to be disturbed."

"We must talk with him, Elder Brother Florn," said Tigg earnestly. "Something has happened that puts him and us in great danger!"

Florn's eyebrows rose. "I'll tell him," he promised. "Let them in, Brother Durvn."

Durvn stepped aside, delighted that the matter had been taken out of his hands. "Come in, then," he invited. "Wait here." He turned and plodded off about his business.

Reepah stirred and lifted his head, peering about. "We are in place of the blue hyoo-mens," he said thickly. "How we ket here?"

Tigg stared at him, noting that his eyes appeared cloudy and that he moved sluggishly. "Are you all right, Reepah?" he questioned anxiously, ignoring the grubber's question. "Are you sick?"

"Not sick," said Reepah. "I ko into *ikkut*—deep sleep of Cold Time. It is thing my people do each year. We cannot help it. We close up our burrows and sleep until spring." He peered about again. "But—I must have dark, quiet place," he said, sounding worried.

Tigg understood; he knew that a number of kinds of animals spent the months of winter in hibernation, and remembered that Reepah had once mentioned that grubbers, too, did this. But this was a new worry, for where could they find a place of safety, where Reepah could sleep in peace, now that Leayzar had soldiers searching for them? "Oh, Reepah," he said sadly, stroking his friend's furry head.

Armindor, followed by Tarbizon, appeared at the far end of the corridor and came hurrying toward them. He knew Tigg well enough to be sure that the boy wasn't prone to exaggerate; if Tigg said they were in danger, then they were in danger, so the magician had left the tremendous events taking place in the Room of Valuables and come to see what was wrong. "What has happened, Tigg?"

"Soldiers who work for Leayzar came to the guestinghouse," Tigg reported. "Leayzar had told them to bring you to him. They're waiting there for you, Armindor. You can't go back." He reached into his smock and brought forth one of the books. "We brought all your books and we have most of our clothes and things."

"Well done," Armindor complimented them. He rubbed his head thoughtfully and sighed. "Well, I fear we really are in trouble. Obviously, Leayzar isn't going to let up. When we don't appear at the guestinghouse by nightfall he'll probably have his men start searching the city for us."

"We'll have to hide somewhere," Jilla suggested. "We'll have to stay in hiding until spring comes and we can sneak out and get on a ship."

"You could stay here," suggested Tarbizon. "You would be perfectly safe. Leayzar wouldn't dare try to take you out of the Sages' Guildhall even if he found out you were here."

"No, but once he did find out we were here, as I am sure he would, he'd have his men waiting to pounce on us the instant we took a step out of the door," Armindor told him. "We have to hide somewhere where he cannot find us."

"That's not going to be easy, I fear," said Tarbizon. "He'll likely have spies looking everywhere for you, and unfortunately you make a rather noticeable group—a tall, stout sage, a boy and a girl, and a talking grubber! You're not much like the everyday folk one sees in Inbal, and that will make you very easy to find, unless you just hole up somewhere and never come out—and even that could draw attention to you from people who might wonder why you are hiding and how it is that you don't have to go out and work for a living."

Jilla's eyes opened wide and her mouth curved into a delighted smile. She had the answer, and now she could pay Armindor back a bit for the help and love he had given her. "I know what to do!" she cried. "We can *change* who we are! Leayzar's men are looking for a sage and a boy and a girl and a grubber, right? Well then, they'd never notice a puppeteer and his two boy helpers! Armindor, if you let your beard grow and put on ordinary clothes, no one would ever know you were a sage, and if I cut my hair short and wore a boy's smock, no one would know I'm a girl. And we can be puppeteers! I have six fine puppets and I know a lot of good plays. Tigg and I could do the shows and you could be the stage manager. No one would ever guess who we really were, and I bet we could even make a lot of money!"

Armindor stared at her thoughtfully. "What about Reepah, though?" he pointed out. "We can't just keep him cooped up out of sight somewhere."

"But yes we can!" Tigg cried out, catching enthusiasm from the girl. "That's exactly what he wants! He just told us, a short time ago, that he needs a dark, quiet place where he can sleep all winter, as grubbers do. We could move into a little house, just as we were going to, and Reepah could stay inside and sleep until spring, and no one would ever see him."

Armindor pursed his lips and looked at Tarbizon. "What do you think? Doesn't seem like a bad idea, does it?"

"I think it's a Roodemiss's laugh of an idea," said Tarbizon, grinning. "I don't think Councilor Leayzar would ever dream that you could change from a big, bald-headed sage and a boy and a girl and a grubber, to a couple of boys and a bearded puppet master. He'd keep his people looking for the magician's company, not a puppeteer's crew!"

"I did want to help with learning the ancient language," said Armindor, "but I guess that would be impossible in any case." He began to grin, looking remarkably like a small boy having a good time. "All right, we shall do it! Here's to the temporary end of the magician's company, and to the beginning of the company of—Gambelan the Puppeteer!"

··· 10 ···

The sky was dull gray, the sun a pale yellow circle, the air crisp and cold. A powder of snow mottled the high-peaked roofs of the buildings forming the great Market Square, and mounds of white lay on every ledge, sill, peak, and projection. Down in the square, the wooden statue of Diormuk, which stood at one end, had a snowy epaulette on each shoulder and a big white turban on its head, while the Fountain of Garmood, at the other end, was fringed with icicles. Winter had settled over Inbal.

The square itself was a muddy yellowish expanse that had been stomped into slush by thousands of pairs of wet and dirty foot coverings and the hoofs and trotters of horses, hornbeasts, squnts, and cattle. In the center of the square a large fire fed by huge logs roared day and night, maintained at public expense to provide warmth for those who needed it, and to light up the square to some extent through the long winter night. For in winter, as in summer, the square was still the main center of social life in Inbal, where people came to buy certain things, to seek out conversation and gossip, to drink and snack, and to be entertained. And all around the square, in winter as in summer, were stationed those who made their living catering to the needs and wants of the people who came to the square—food vendors with glowing grills; dispensers of beer and spirits from casks and barrels; blue-robed sage fortune-tellers; sellers of finely crafted stone knife blades, saws, and axe heads; sellers of stone, bone, and wooden beads, bracelets, and rings and decorative plugs for ears, noses, and lips; priestly sellers of prayer sticks, religious statues, and charms against deadwalkers and evil spirits; and jugglers, clowns, minstrels, and puppeteers.

One group of puppeteers was the highly popular Gambelan Company, newcomers to the square who were said to have fled from the war-torn Land of Wemms and were making their new home in Inbal. Gambelan was a big, hearty man with a thick mop of white hair and stubbly white beard, and his "company" consisted of two boys named Tib and Jorl. They presented their entertainments from a boxlike wooden stage beneath a broad cloth awning, and their popularity stemmed from two causes. One was that people could crowd under the awning and watch a play for only one iron bit, the smallest-value coin there was, and only half the amount charged by other puppeteers. The other was that they had departed from the standard puppet plays that had been performed for a hundred years and more, before many generations, and instead offered exciting new productions featuring a horridly hateful villain as a central character—a ratlike creature known as Reen, who sought to make all the other characters his slaves but was always thwarted by a brave, handsome hero called the Reenkiller.

It had been Jilla—now Jorl—who had conceived the idea of using the puppet shows to help make the people of Inbal aware of the danger from the reen, as Armindor had hoped to do. Over their first meal in the little house they had taken, a stew of dried fruits and meat in a rich broth, prepared by Armindor, Jilla presented her plan to the magician and his apprentice.

"I've been thinking," she announced, delving into her bowl with a wooden spoon. "Lots and lots of people are going to see our puppet shows during the winter. Maybe there's a way you could let all of them know about the reen."

Armindor paused in his eating and eyed her with interest. In the privacy of the house he had taken off the white horsehair wig that had been obtained for him, but the beard that was sprouting on his chin and cheeks nevertheless made him seem very different to the two youngsters, "What do you mean?" he asked.

"Well, you couldn't come right out and tell them, of course," said the girl. She and Tigg had both had their hair cropped close and they, too, looked oddly different. "But what if we talked about the reen in the plays? What if we had reen *in* some of the plays? We could make them very nasty and cruel and sneaky, so that people would know what they are really like."

"People wouldn't know they were real, though," objected Tigg. "They would just be characters in a play."

"That might not matter," said Armindor thoughtfully. "After we are safely away from here, in the spring, Tarbizon is going to have all the Inbal sages begin warning people about the reen, and if some people are already familiar with the idea of an evil, intelligent, ratlike creature, it might make things easier. Perhaps we should do it."

"It could be dangerous," Tigg warned. "What if Leayzar were to hear about it? He'd know it was us right away!"

"I don't think there's much chance of that," Armindor assured him. "I'm very sure, for several reasons, that Leayzar has never mentioned the reen to any of his soldiers or any of the people he might have searching for us, so even if some of those people should come to our plays and see a reen puppet, they wouldn't think anything of it and wouldn't bother to report it to him. And you certainly don't have to worry about *him* ever coming to any of our plays; he'll spend the winter in the palace, in front of the fire with a mug of berry beer in his hand, like all the rest of the nobles, and never come near any place where common people are having fun."

So, after a bit more discussion, Jilla-Jorl's idea was adopted. Armindor, in his white wig and with his beard several days longer, had gone to a woodcarver and hired him to produce a head for a reen puppet. "It's to be an evil character in some of our plays," he told the man. "Make it look like a snarling rat with a large round head and a humanlike chin."

Working together, the three of them revised a standard puppet play that Jilla was familiar with, fitting the reen puppet into it. The play was called "The Wicked Moneylender," and the role of the moneylender was always given to the scowling-faced puppet that most puppeteers called by the name of "Nasty," but in the Gambelan Company version the role now went to the reen puppet. In the original, the wicked moneylender was beaten at the end by the character called Hero, wielding a stick between his arms, which were the puppeteer's fingers. But Armindor felt that the audience should be made to realize that the reen was such a dangerous creature it had to be killed, and he constructed a spear out of a crossbow arrow, which could be slipped into Hero's hand and with which the human puppet could stab the reen puppet.

The play, retitled "The Evil Reen," became an instant success, with Jilla playing the role of Beauty, the heroine, in a girlish voice and the reen in a throaty, snarling voice, and Tigg taking the parts of the sage, the clown, and Hero, who had been renamed "Reenkiller." Armindor acted as prompter and stage manager, helping the two youngsters get puppets quickly off and on their arms and handing them props as needed. After a few days the space under the awning (specially made by a sailmaker) was invariably sold out for both the afternoon and evening performances, as word spread quickly that a totally new puppet play was being offered in the square, at a delightfully low cost.

But while the puppet plays were now a major part of their life, Armindor and Tigg still kept abreast of the work the sages of Inbal were doing in learning the ancient language of the Age of Magic. They had decided it would be best not to return to the guildhall, much as they wished to, in case it was being watched Leayzar's soldiers or spies. And so, with Tarbizon they had worked out a furtive system of keeping in touch and passing information. Every few days, Brother Florn, Sister Chuveen, or Tarbizon himself would pass through the square around midmorning, always pausing for a moment at the statue of Diormuk to tighten a leg wrapping, adjust a hood, or perform some other quick task. Tigg or Jilla would be lounging nearby, and a few quick words would be whispered to them. That night, Armindor, Tigg, and Jilla would walk to a certain street, stop at a certain door, and after looking around to make sure they weren't being spied on, slip inside. There, in Tarbizon's home, while his pleasant wife gave them a good dinner, they would learn what had been gained from the fantastic box to which, day and night, groups of sages were listening and writing down the words spoken and their meanings as shown by the pictures on the gray square. Other sages were now making copies of the words and meanings that had been taken down so far, and still others were beginning to study and memorize the list. All this was being done secretly, with every sage sworn not to speak of it to anyone outside the Guild.

"I wish I could be helping, instead of hiding behind a puppet stage with my head shrouded in this Rood-emiss-cursed wig," Armindor grumbled during one of these sessions. He scrubbed at his chin. "This beard itches, too!" Then he grinned. "But you know, Tarbizon, by making us go into hiding, Leayzar has actually helped me do what I hoped to do in the first place! People are learning about the reen from the puppet shows. They are beginning to talk about the creatures. Just yesterday I heard one woman tell another that she had chased a rat as big as a reen out of her pantry, and instead of playing Thieves and Peacekeepers, little children are playing Reens and Reenkillers. I don't think I could have done as well if I'd been permitted to stand in the square and give a speech!"

The days passed and the winter wore on. The day of the Feast of the New Fire arrived, the shortest day of the year, when at sunrise everyone kindled a New Year's Fire from the embers of the old one, and at sunset everyone lit as many candles and oil lamps as they could afford to burn and prepared the finest feast they could, in an ancient ritual designed to give courage against the cold and gloom of winter and to urge the gods and spirits to send back the sun. Thereafter, each morning, sages who specialized in knowledge of the sky climbed the stairs to the top of the East Tower of the city walls and checked the position of the rising sun to make sure it was making the return journey that would again bring it close enough to the world to melt the ice and snow and bring the plants back to life. On the farms scattered outside the city, farmers began to scan the snow on the ground for footprints and other signs that hibernating animals had awakened, for this meant that spring would surely come. The days grew noticeably longer, for while the great Clock of the Falling Sand in the main worship house of Garmood had been filled to only seven marks at sunset on the day of the Feast of the New Fire, sunset now found it filled to more than eight—and then nine. In the little house where Armindor, Tigg, and Jilla were staying, Reepah began to come awake for lengthening periods. And finally, one morning, the city of Inbal awoke to the sound of distant rumbling and thudding and an occasional loud, thunderous crack, which were the noises of ice breaking up on the Silver Sea. Spring was definitely coming.

"I think I should go to the docks and see if I can get us onto one of the first ships away from here," Armindor told the children and the now wide-awake Reepah. "I'll be back in plenty of time for the first show."

Swathed in a heavy brown cloak and with his hood

pulled well down, he plodded through the slushy streets. Reaching the dock area, he paused to look carefully about. He was sure that if Councilor Leayzar was still interested in capturing him, Leayzar would sooner or later think of having the docks watched, knowing that Armindor and the children would probably try to get away from Inbal by sea. Armindor saw no one suspicious, so he moved toward the beached ships, where groups of seamen were working. Shortly he was directed to the master of a particular vessel, with whom he talked for a time. A satisfactory agreement was soon reached, and Armindor turned to leave. Once more he looked about carefully, to make sure he was not being observed with undue interest by anyone. All seemed well, and he strode off.

Armindor had been quite right in thinking that the docks might be watched. However, he had looked for a human watcher. The eyes that had observed his coming, from a shadowed depression beneath a beached ship, and the ears that had listened to his conversation with the sea captain were not human. And even had he turned to look back, Armindor probably would not have noticed the small furtive shape that, keeping to the shadows and making quick darts from hiding place to hiding place, followed him as he made his way back to the Market Square.

···11···

Armindor entered the Market Square and headed straight for the puppet theater, where Jilla and Tigg were getting things ready for the afternoon performance. From a distance, his follower watched him come to a halt and begin to talk to the two youngsters. After a few moments, it turned and made a quick run for the nearby Fountain of Garmood. At one point, where the base of the fountain rested on the dirt street, were some loose, separated stones behind which was the dark orifice of a hole. Armindor's follower slipped between the stones and vanished from sight.

"It's all arranged," Armindor told Tigg and Jilla in a low voice. "We shall be leaving in eight days' time." He glanced around. "Now, we don't want any of our neighbors here to know we're leaving, because that might start talk about us that could reach the ears of Leayzar's spies and start them thinking. So we'll keep all our preparations secret and just keep on doing as we have been, the three of us giving puppet shows and Reepah staying out of sight, until the very last moment."

Tigg and Jilla exchanged worried glances that Armindor caught instantly. "What is the matter?" he asked sharply.

"Well—Reepah has been begging to get out of the house," Tigg told him. "Now that his winter sleep is over he's wide awake and wants to be active. I don't think he could stand being cooped up for eight more days! He wants to come here and see what we're doing,"

"But we don't dare let him be seen!" Armindor protested. "There's not another grubber in Inbal. It would be like lighting a signal fire for Councilor Leayzar, to show him where we are!"

Tigg nodded unhappily. But at that moment a workman passed by, carrying a long wooden toolbox by a leather strap. The shape of the box made Tigg think of the traveling couch in which he had taken his enforced ride as a captive, and suddenly an idea popped into his head. "I know what we can do! We could carry Reepah in a toolbox like that man has. We could cut slots in it, like a traveling couch has, so he could breathe and see out. We could keep him in the theater with us, and make a tiny hole so he could look at things."

Armindor fingered his beard, a habit he had unknowingly picked up from Tarbizon. "I guess that would be all right."

That evening, after the last performance, the three went to the Street of Cabinetmakers and purchased a large toolbox, having the carpenter cut slots in each side. The next day, to Reepah's great satisfaction, he was carried to the square and set free inside the puppet theater.

It was a chilly but pleasant day, and the square was

more crowded than it had been since the beginning of winter. Armindor took up his post at the end of the awning and began collecting coins from those who wanted to watch the puppet play, ushering patrons to a place under the awning, with firstcomers being placed closest to the stage. As usual, the audience was made up mainly of children and their mothers, but there were always a few men in attendance: merchant apprentices and secretaries who were killing time while their masters did business nearby, cart drivers whose animals were being fed, and others with a little time on their hands. There were usually two to three soldiers of the High Chairman's peacekeeping force patrolling the square, and whenever one of these showed interest, Armindor would offer him a place under the awning at no charge. It was useful to be on good terms with Peacekeepers.

When he judged that there was no more room for anyone beneath the awning, Armindor turned and made his way back to the theater. This was actually just a tall, boxlike structure that he'd had built by a carpenter, under Jilla's instructions, when he and the children had first taken on the role of puppeteers. A square opening in the upper third of the side of the box facing the awning was the actual stage where the puppets performed; inside the box, which one entered through a door, Tigg and Jilla stood on a bench and stretched up their arms with the puppets on them, putting the little "actors" on the stage in view of the audience. Armindor stood behind the two, to hand them props and help them on and off with puppets. Today, Reepah was crouched at one end of the bench, peeking through a little hole that Tigg had gouged for him.

The first act of "The Evil Reen" began, and Armindor marveled, as he always did, at the skill and exuberance of the two youngsters. He had expected Jilla to be an experienced performer, but had been rather surprised at how easily Tigg had become an accomplished puppeteer. Apparently the boy's early years in the streets of Ingarron, when he'd lived by his wits, had turned him into a skillful actor who wasn't the least bit put off at performing for an audience.

When the first act came to its end, Armindor stepped outside to stretch his legs. Standing at the edge of the theater he glanced idly about. Abruptly, he stiffened.

A small crowd of men had entered the square at the far end, and they were moving purposefully, all bunched together, toward the part of the square where the Gambelan puppet theater stood. It looked to Armindor as if most of them were mercenary soldiers. But one man . . .

Digging into an inner pocket of his cloak, Armindor took out the Spell of Far-seeing, which he carried with him at all times. It wouldn't matter if anyone nearby should see him using it; they wouldn't have any idea of what it was and would probably think he was simply treating a sore eye with a charm of some sort. But whether anyone saw him using it or not, he had to find out if his fears were justified. Lifting the red tube to his eye, he adjusted it until the image was sharp and clear. He looked at the approaching group of men and a face jumped out at him.

As he had feared, it was Councilor Leayzar. The man's sharp features were set in a grim expression, and he seemed to be looking straight into Armindor's eyes. The magician knew that Leayzar couldn't possibly make him out at this distance, but it was obvious that the man was staring at the puppet theater and that was where he was headed. Half a dozen soldiers were with him, and at his side was a portly man in servant's clothing, carrying a wooden box that instantly drew Armindor's attention. It was almost a twin of the box he'd had made to carry Reepah in, and he could see the slots that were cut into its sides.

He went cold. Thrusting the spell back into his cloak, he jerked open the theater door and opened his mouth to speak. But the squeaky voice of Reepah stopped him. The grubber was facing Tigg and Jilla, who were staring at him with concerned expressions.

"An *isst*—a reen—I say!" The grubber was waving his arms in agitation. "Coming toward us. Ketting nearer! The smell is strong!"

"He's right," said Armindor. "Leayzar has found us. He has soldiers, and there's a man with him carrying a box with a reen in it. We've got to try to get away!"

"A reen?" Tigg said in astonishment. "Leayzar has a *reen?*"

"He is working with them," Armindor explained. "That was what questioned you in that cellar, Tigg—a reen. But come now, they're almost here!"

Tigg thought swiftly. He knew that Armindor would never be able to outrun a group of strong young soldiers, and he cringed in horror at the thought of what Leayzar—and *reen*—might do to the magician if they got hold of him. But there was a chance. . . .

"Go, quick," he ordered. "I can hold them off while you get away. Go to the guildhall. I'll meet you there."

Armindor stared at him, appalled. "But—"

"It's you they want, not me," cried Tigg. "I'll be all right, believe me. Now go. Go!" He snatched up the

Reenkiller puppet, slid it onto his arm, hopped onto the bench, and lifted his arm so that the puppet suddenly popped into the view of the audience, leaning out toward them.

"People of Inbal!" shouted the boy. "You know me. I am the Reenkiller! And I bring you dreadful news! This very moment—*there is a reen among you!* I am going to come out and show it to you."

Now Armindor's thoughts were racing. He realized what Tigg was trying to do—create a diversion so that the others could get away. He knew Tigg was clever enough to make it work, and nimble enough to get away himself, but the sage was terrified to think that the boy might be hurt or even killed. He knew that he couldn't help his apprentice, he was too old and slow to do any fighting, and if he stayed and tried to help he might simply ruin whatever chance Tigg had.

"Roodemiss watch over you, Tigg," he moaned. He motioned to Jilla, "Take Reepah. Come!"

The audience had reacted to Tigg's Reenkiller announcement with delight. They thought, of course, that this was all part of the play, and found it tremendously interesting and exciting. What was going to happen, they wondered; how would the puppet prove its statement? The puppet had flashed out of sight after making its announcement, and now they waited to see what "he" would do next.

Tigg quickly swathed himself in his cloak so that most of his head and body were covered and only his eyes showed. With the arm wearing the Reenkiller upraised, he stepped out of the theater and confronted the audience, which greeted him with cheers. Looking past them he saw Councilor Leayzar, the soldiers, and the man with the box, approaching, no more than fifty steps away.

Tigg lifted the Reenkiller puppet high and wiggled his finger so that the little figure appeared to be waving its spear. "People of Inbal, follow me," shouted the boy, making his voice as deep and heroic as he could. "I will show you where the vile and treacherous reen is hiding!"

He moved into the crowd, heading toward Leayzar. Instantly he was surrounded by a swirl of excited children, their eyes shining, their mouths round O's of delight, their hands stretched out to try to touch the Reenkiller. Their mothers, some giggling with embarrassment to have become part of such an odd event, kept pace with them, and the men in the audience, curious and interested at this development in the puppet play, followed along.

At the sight of a crowd of some thirty or more people suddenly surging toward him, Councilor Leayzar stopped in his tracks, and his servant and soldiers automatically followed suit. Leayzar could only stare for a moment, mouth hanging open in astonishment, but then he realized that the crowd represented an impediment to his plan of catching Armindor by surprise and capturing him. Leayzar's thin face reddened in anger and he made a sweeping motion with his arm, as if he were clearing a cluster of dirty dishes off a table. "Out of our way!" he bawled. "Make way, I tell you!"

Few if any of the ordinary people of Inbal ever attended meetings of the High Council, so Leayzar was unrecognized by everyone in the crowd save Tigg. He was not wearing any of the face jewelry affected by most nobles, and he was clad in a plain cloak, like the brown and gray cloaks of the commoners, rather than a colorful, expensive russet or blue garment, so it was not evident that he was a noble. Those who took any notice of him at all probably thought he was merely a well-to-do merchant who had hired a handful of soldiers to guard his money, which was being carried by a servant, but for the most part he was simply ignored by the majority of the crowd, which had their eyes on Tigg. With Tigg leading them, they flowed right up to Leayzar, stopping when the boy did.

"The reen is hiding in this box," announced Tigg, moving his finger so that the Reenkiller pointed with his tiny spear. "Tell them to open the box and you will see that I speak the truth."

At the word *reen* Leayzar's face twisted into an expression of dismay and he stared in horror at the puppet. But the man carrying the box reached out with one hand and twitched the cloak away from Tigg's face. "It's the magician's apprentice!" he hissed.

"What?" Leayzar's eyes flashed from the puppet to the boy, and his expression changed to one of rage. "You're right, Pan!" He gestured at one of his soldiers who stood near Tigg. "Seize this boy."

The soldier took a step forward and clamped his fingers around Tigg's shoulder. "Make them open the box!" shouted Tigg. "I, the Reenkiller, pledge that there is a reen in that box." No matter what happens now, at least Armindor and Jilla and Reepah are safely away, thought the boy. But perhaps I can turn the tables on Leayzar. "Open the box," he cried again, and started a steady chant. "Open the box, open the box."

The children took up the chant immediately "Open the box," shrilled a chorus of young voices. Some of the mothers joined in as well as several of the men, feeling this was all some great jest they were participating in. They were delighted with the novelty of this entertainment; it was well worth a single iron bit.

Leayzar lost his head. Teeth clenched, he stepped forward and slapped Tigg a savage blow that rocked the boy's head back and brought a trickle of blood from his nose. "Shut your mouth," snarled the noble.

The children instantly fell silent, and several of the women gave exclamations of anger. A burly squnt driver pushed out of the crowd and confronted Leayzar. "What was that for?" he demanded. "It's all just in fun." But as he regarded the expressions on the faces of the noble and his servant, he became aware that there was more to the situation than a mere joke. "Here, what *have* you got in that box?" he questioned suspiciously.

"Stay out of this or you'll have to pick up your teeth," threatened the soldier who had hold of Tigg, hoping to impress his employer, the councilor. The squnt driver swung around to face him.

"Is that a fact now?" he said mildly, and brought his knee suddenly and savagely up into the soldier's groin. The soldier made a sound like a squalling cat and doubled over, letting go of the boy.

Tigg saw his chance. The crowd was on his side entirely, and Leayzar and his soldiers were disconcerted. Saying a silent prayer to Roodemiss-Who-Watches-Over-Sages, Durbis-Who-Watches-Over-Thieves, and Garmood-Who-Watches-Over-All, asking that Armindor and Reepah be right about the reen in the box, Tigg took two quick steps forward and kicked the box out of the hands of Leayzar's servant. It sailed upward in an arc, turning over twice in midair, and hit the frozen dirt of the street with a crash that broke the lid off.

A reen rolled out.

The creature was stunned from the impact of its fall, which was probably equal to a fall from a second-floor window for a human, and it could only blink and stare groggily as it tried to push itself to its feet. Inasmuch as it had been hidden from sight and had no need to try to pass itself off as an ordinary rat, as it had done while following Armindor, it was dressed in the way of the reen. A skin pouch hung from its neck by a thong, and around its waist was a colorful cloth belt from which hung a sheathed dagger. It was obviously no dull-witted, dirty, scampering street rat!

At the sight of it there was a single concerted ear-splitting scream from all the children in the crowd gathered around Tigg and Leayzar's party. Here was the monster of the puppet plays, the hated creature of evil, in live flesh. A few of the younger children backed away from it, clutching at their mothers' cloaks, but the others, almost instinctively, were drawn to destroy this thing that they clearly perceived as a threat. They converged on the reen, attacking it with feet and fists. It tried to squirm away, but the kicks and blows and the incredible din of the steady, high-pitched shrieking of its assailants dazed it even more. Then a child struck it savagely on the head with a toy spear carved from a piece of wood, stretching it motionless on the ground.

"Hold," yelled a commanding voice. A pair of the High Chairman's Peacekeepers, drawn by the shrieks and commotion, were pushing in among the children, who fell silent and melted back out of the way. The two soldiers stared down at the ratlike form on the ground, and one of them prodded it with the point of his spear. When it showed no sign of life he bent down, picked it up gingerly by the tail, and straightened up, holding it at arm's length and staring at it in astonishment.

"By Maldum," he said, invoking the name of the battle god worshiped by most soldiers, "it's the reen! Like in the puppet plays, Dorvn. But it's real!"

"Real as a mug of beer," marveled his companion. Both men had often been Armindor's guests at the puppet theater and were well acquainted with the reen character. Dorvn tugged the little dagger out of the sheath on the reen's belt and peered at it. "Maldum! This is made out of *metal!*" His tone was incredulous, for the small amounts of workable metal that had been left by the wasteful ancient culture destroyed in the nuclear wars of the twenty-first century were now used only for coins and jewelry; to find a weapon made of metal was like finding one made of a precious jewel.

"Where did this creature come from?" asked the first soldier, hefting the body of the reen and addressing the crowd.

"It was in the box," the burly squnt driver volunteered. "It was in a box that this fellow was—why, he's gone."

Tigg glanced about. It was true; Leayzar and his servant had both vanished. With his attention on the reen, he hadn't seen them go, but he realized that once the reen had been uncovered the two must have fled to avoid any questions.

"They know about it," said the squnt driver, indicating the soldier who had been with Leayzar. "They were with the man who had the box, and the other fellow."

"What's this all about, Captain?" said the Peacekeeper named Dorvn, addressing the question to one of the soldiers whose leather helmet displayed the two red feathers of captain's rank. "Who was the man with the box?"

"It was Pan Biblo, the top servant of Councilor Leayzar," said the captain. He licked his lips, frowning. "I didn't know that thing was in the box—none of us did. The councilor brought us here to arrest a group of puppeteers for some reason, and Pan came along carrying the box. That's all I know."

"Councilor Leayzar?" said Peacekeeper Dorvn, frowning. He looked at his companion. "Something stinks here, Marl!"

The other nodded. "I think so, too. The High Chairman better hear about all this." Without further word they turned and strode off, Marl still holding the dead reen dangling by its tail. Tigg watched them for a moment, bubbling inside with elation. Then without even removing the puppet from his arm, he turned and began to run in the direction that had been taken by Jilla, Reepah, and Armindor, eager to catch up with them and tell them that the danger from Leayzar had been thwarted.

··· 12 ···

"I don't think anyone is coming after us," said Jilla, looking over her shoulder. "I don't see anyone." They were on the Street of Bakers, and the aroma of fresh-baked bread hung enticingly in the air. Except for two bearers carrying a traveling couch in the opposite direction from which Armindor and Jilla were going, the street was empty.

"Good," puffed Armindor, slowing to a walk from the ponderous and not-too-rapid trot he had been maintaining. "I'm too old and stout to keep up such a pace for very long." He, too, glanced back over his shoulder. "No sign of Tigg yet."

"He'll show up soon," said Jilla.

"I hope so!" Armindor was berating himself for having left the boy. I should have stayed and faced Leayzar with him whether he wanted me to or not, he thought. He's quick and clever, but he is only a boy, and Leayzar and six soldiers may have been too much for him to handle.

The man and the girl, with Reepah riding on her shoulder, made their way up several more streets, finally turning into the Street of Sages and heading toward the massive guildhall that loomed over the smaller dwellings forming the two sides of the street. Armindor jerked the leather cord hanging by the entrance, making the gong inside go *tunka-tunka-tunka*. The door was opened by the chubby young sage, Durvn. "Yes?" he said, not recognizing Armindor in his Gambelan disguise.

Realizing this, Armindor snatched the wig from his head and tapped his blue earring. "It's I, High Master Armindor of Ingarron. I must see High Master Tarbizon."

Once again, Brother Durvn found himself in a quandary. Even though no one but high-ranking sages wore the little round blue earrings, he still didn't recognize this white-bearded man wearing a brown cloak instead of a blue sage's robe. He dared not let in a stranger, yet he dared not risk offending someone who might truly be his superior. He looked around helplessly and caught sight of a figure coming out of one of the rooms that opened onto the long hallway of the carved wooden walls and pebbled floor. "Elder Sister Chuveen! Can you come here, please?"

"Eh?" Chuveen padded toward him, peered through the open door, and caught sight of Jilla and Armindor, both of whom she recognized from having carried communications to them at the square. "High Master Armindor!" she exclaimed.

Durvn's problem was solved. Quickly he bowed, hand to forehead and palm out, in the prescribed manner. "Please enter, High Master," he said, beaming and stepping back.

Armindor and Jilla stepped into the hallway. "Is High Master Tarbizon here?" questioned Armindor of Chuveen.

"He is down in the Room of Valuables, watching the work being done on the words spoken by the voice from the box," Chuveen answered. "I will tell him you are here." She padded off.

"The box is still talking then," marveled Jilla, who had been told all about the box by Armindor, and had listened while he and Tigg frequently discussed it at the supper table.

"Yes. There are thousands of words in a language, and one must know most of them in order to fully understand the language," said Armindor. "The box has given us thousands already, but there must be many thousands more to go." He sighed deeply, and the girl knew what his thoughts were; he had made the difficult decision to leave the box in Inbal when he and the children escaped, so that the Inbal sages could continue the important work of learning the ancient language. But with a start, she suddenly realized that perhaps they wouldn't be able to escape from Inbal now that Leayzar had spoiled their plans.

Tarbizon appeared, hurrying toward them. "Armindor! What has happened? Why are you here?"

"We were discovered," Armindor told him glumly. "Leayzar came into the square with his soldiers this afternoon. Tigg caused a diversion so that Jilla and Reepah and I could get away. I hope to Roodemiss that *he* was able to get away!"

"This is bad news, Brother," exclaimed Tarbizon. "Even if your apprentice did get away, and I pray to Roodemiss he did, Leayzar will be after you like a woodsdog after a meadowhopper!" He smacked his fist into his palm. "What a pity! Only a few more days and you probably could have been on a ship, safely away from here."

"The arrangements were all made," Armindor acknowledged.

Tunk went the wooden gong by the door, and they all gave startled little jumps.

"Tick!" said Reepah, scrambling down Jilla's body to the floor. "It is Tick!"

Not waiting for young Durvn, whose current duty was to answer the door, Tarbizon stepped toward it and lifted the wooden bar. He opened the door to reveal Tigg standing in the alcove. The boy's face broke into a grin as he saw his friends. Reepah swarmed up onto his shoulder and hugged his head, Jilla threw her arms around him, and a much-relieved Armindor pummeled his arm. "What happened?" the magician asked.

Tigg came into the hall, swaggering just a trifle. "Well, I became the Reenkiller! I led the crowd against Leayzar and his bully soldiers and demanded that the box Pan Biblo was carrying be opened. A scuffle started between one of the men on my side and one of Leayzar's soldiers, and I managed to kick the box out of Biblo's hand. It broke open and there was a reen in it, just as you said. It tried to get away, but all the children fell upon it and killed it, Garmood bless 'em! Just then, two of the High Chairman's Peacekeepers showed up, who knew all about the reen from our puppet shows. Leayzar and Pan Biblo ran away, and the Peacekeepers took the dead reen to show to the High Chairman!"

Tarbizon looked from the boy to Armindor. "Brother, this is a wonderul turn of events! High Chairman Joreo would never have listened to us if we'd brought him a dead reen and told him it came out of a box that one of Councilor Leayzar's people was carrying, but he'll believe two of his Peacekeepers! When he sees a reen that was picked up in Market Square of his own city, he'll know you were telling the truth about the creatures, and he's sure to want to talk with you again. You can tell him all about Leayzar, and I suspect that will be the end of the councilor. This could be the answer to all your problems, Armindor!"

As Tarbizon was speaking, Reepah, squatting on Tigg's shoulder, suddenly stiffened. Releasing his gentle grip on the boy's head, the grubber turned and, with his nostrils flaring, leaned out to one side to peer through the doorway, which had been left partly open when Tigg came in. It was early evening now, and the houses across the street from the guildhall were black silhouettes against an orange sky in which the sun was setting. The street was filling with shadows.

"*Isst!*" shrieked the grubber, using the word of his kind for the reen. "Many coming! Close the door! Close the door!"

It was a moment before any of the startled humans could act, then Armindor, who was standing nearest the door, threw his weight against it to slam it shut and dropped the bar into place. "What is it, Reepah? What is happening?"

The grubber's nostrils were quivering and his lip was curled back in a snarl. "Many, many *isst*. Reen. Outside. The air is filled with their ukly smell!"

"I don't understand. You mean they are coming *here*?" exclaimed Tarbizon.

"Here *now*," stated Reepah. "Many!"

"Listen!" cried Jilla, pointing toward the door. In the

· 107 ·

quick silence following her cry the others, too, heard the little scratchings and chopping sounds coming from the door, as if many small knife points and axes were being used to gouge through it.

"They're making an attack," snarled Armindor. "We know they want the spells from the Age of Magic; they must have discovered the spells are here and they're going to try to take them by force. I feared something like this!"

"How can we fight them?" asked Tarbizon, staring at the door. "There isn't a weapon in the whole building."

"We can't fight them, they will simply shoot us all with their blow-tubes," Armindor told him. "Our only hope is to keep them out of here."

"It will take them a while to get through the door, and they'll probably try to find other ways of getting in," warned Tigg, his dark eyes blazing with excitement. "They can climb; they'll probably try to get in through any windows."

Tarbizon stared about wildly, filled with fear for the safety of his beloved guildhall and all its arts and treasures, as well as for the lives of the sages under his leadership. His eyes fell upon Brother Durvn, who stood nearby goggle-eyed and open-mouthed, trying to figure out what was happening. "Durvn! Alert all the sages that we are being attacked. Tell them to make sure every window is shut and barred. Tell them to come here with any kind of weapon they can find. Move!" Durvn rushed off, howling.

Armindor was eyeing the door. "We could delay them further if we pushed a table or something in front of the door," he suggested.

Tarbizon indicated a nearby room. "In here." The

two men and the boy and girl wrestled a large heavy table out of the room and pushed it flat against the door.

The guildhall was now filled with sounds of excited voices and rushing feet. By twos and threes the sages who had come to the guildhall this day to study, to experiment, to work on pet projects, swarmed into the hall armed with an odd assortment of makeshift weapons: shaving knives, fireplace pokers, hammers. They shouted questions. "Who is attacking us, High Master?" "Have those Roodemiss-cursed squnts from Wemms brought their war here?"

"Brothers! Sisters!" Tarbizon raised his arms to quiet the noise and confusion. He spoke rapidly, his voice high-pitched with excitement. "You all know of the reen, the ratlike creatures discovered by High Master Armindor of Ingarron and his apprentice. An army of these creatures is attacking the guildhall. They want the spells from the Age of Magic that we hold in safekeeping. Our only hope is to keep them out, for if they get in, they will kill us all and take whatever they want!" There was a shocked murmur from the blue-robed people. "Spread out through the building, on this floor and the next. Watch all the windows. Block them with furniture if you can. If any reen do get in, try to kill them. Don't let them point their little blow-tubes at you!" He waved his arms. "Go, everyone. Roodemiss be with us all."

Some in fear, some in anger, some puzzled and uncertain, and some grinning with excitement, the sages of Inbal, from oldsters like Sister Chuveen to the stalwart young Brother Florn, rushed to defend their guildhall. Armindor, Tigg, and Jilla, and Tarbizon and two other sages, stayed near the entrance door.

"Could they get in through the walls anywhere?" wondered Armindor, running his hand over a carved panel.

Tarbizon shook his head. "I think not. The outer logs are thicker than your body, Armindor, and there is a layer of plaster behind them and this wooden paneling atop that."

"Then they'll likely keep at the door or climb up and try the windows, as Tigg says," said Armindor. "If we can keep them out until morning comes I think they will leave, for I don't believe they are ready to try to take over the whole city yet, and they wouldn't want to be seen making an attack such as this."

"Maybe someone will come down the street tonight and see them and go to the Peacekeepers for help," said Jilla.

"I pray that no one does come down this street tonight, Little Maid, for the reen would surely kill them," the magician told her. He shook his head, "We cannot count on any help. We must keep them out until morning comes."

But these words were no sooner out of his mouth than there was a sudden commotion of bumps and shouts and running footsteps overhead from the second floor. A blue-robed figure came rushing down the stairway at the far end of the hall. It was the chubby Brother Durvn.

"High Master, they're inside!" he bawled. "They got in through the roof. They've killed Nabon and Sister Potl!"

"Roodemiss!" groaned Tarbizon. "Quick, everyone into the Room of Valuables," he shouted in the next breath.

Sages, Jilla and Tigg with them, streamed toward the opposite end of the hall, where a stairway led down into the cellar. Tarbizon positioned himself at the head of the stairs, peering down the hallway to make sure everyone reached safety. "This way," he shouted at the handful of blue robes that came rushing down from the second floor. But even as these people sprinted down the hallway, the last of them flung up his arms and pitched headlong to lie motionless on the pebbled floor. Tarbizon saw that reen were moving down the far stairway, sending poisoned darts after the fleeing sages.

"Quickly, quickly," he urged, and as the last of the sages turned down the stairway, Tarbizon followed, hearing the *snick* of a dart striking the paneled wall where he had stood a moment before. The last to pass through the entrance into the Room of Valuables, he whirled and tugged the heavy door shut, dropping the bar into place across it. He looked down to see a crowd of anxious faces looking up from the bottom of the stairs. "There are no sages alive up there," he said grimly. "May Roodemiss look after their spirits" He plodded wearily down the stairs, gestured toward a tall, heavy wooden cabinet nearby. "Some of you help push that up against the door."

He made his way through the crowd to where Armindor and the two children stood. "It would take them days to chop through that door and the cabinet. We should be all right here until morning."

But Armindor shook his head. "I fear that is no longer true, Brother. They are inside the building now, and cannot be seen by any passersby in the streets. They can take all the time they need, now, to break through to us."

Dismay showed on Tarbizon's face as he realized the truth of Armindor's words; realized that there was now no hope. He stared for a moment at the sober faces of Tigg and Jilla, then turned to look at his sages. Many of them were looking toward him and Armindor, probably wondering what the two were saying to each other. Others were talking in low voices, some were watching the doorway, where the big cabinet now lay on its side on the stairs, its top jammed against the door. Through the low hum of conversation could be heard the voice of the box from the Age of Magic, still pronouncing words in the ancient tongue. "Wheel. Wheel—wheel—wheel—wheel."

Jilla understood, from what Armindor had said, that she was going to die. She was rather surprised to find that she wasn't much afraid. She might have been afraid, she felt, if the form of death were to be painful, but she had heard Armindor once describe how the poisoned darts of the reen killed instantly. So, at least it wouldn't hurt. And at least she would be dying well fed and among loved ones, rather than alone and starving, as might have happened if she had not met Armindor, Tigg, and Reepah on the road in Wemms that day many moons ago. She was sorry that she would never have the chance to grow up and have a husband and children, but that was not the fate that had been given her, so she had to accept whatever happened. After she was dead she would be a spirit, of course, and she could search for the spirits of Hemm, Ola, and Anjin, and she could introduce them to the spirits of Armindor, Tigg, and Reepah, who would probably be with her. She was sure they would all like each other, and she and they would probably all have good times in the spirit world—at least, that was what the priests of Garmood promised.

She glanced at Tigg and wondered what he was thinking about. Actually, Tigg too was thinking about their situation, but he refused to consider death as a possibility. He had been in tight places before and gotten out of them, and he and his friends would get out of this, too! Durbis, the spirit-god of thieves, to whose worship Tigg had been introduced at a very early age, taught that one should use one's wits, and that was what Tigg intended to do. There was surely some way of thwarting the reen! Perhaps everyone in the cellar could break through one of the walls and dig a tunnel up to freedom while the reen were still trying to get through the door. Perhaps they could arm themselves with torches and make a fiery charge through the reen! Perhaps— The boy's eyes roamed over the room, seeking a surefire way of saving himself and all the others.

Suddenly from the doorway came the sound of a series of muffled thuds. Silence fell as every head turned to look at the door. Had the reen devised some quick way of breaking in?

Armindor made his way to the table on which sat the talking box. He stared down at the marvelous object for a moment. Then in a loud voice he cried out, "I will not let them have this! I will not let those ratspawn have the magic of our ancestors to use against our own people. I will destroy it first!"

Picking up a heavy stool, he swung it up over his head and set himself to bring it down in a smashing blow that would crush the wonderful talking box from the Age of Magic.

··· 13 ···

"Wait!" One of the sages nearest the door stretched an imploring hand toward Armindor. "I think—I thought I heard human voices!"

There was total silence, except for the soft voice coming from the box, as every person in the room strained to listen. After a few moments there was another succession of thuds on the door, which, it seemed to Jilla, sounded like someone pounding with a fist. Then everyone clearly heard the sound of a shouting voice, muffled by the thickness of the door.

"We're saved!" exclaimed the sage by the door, his voice breaking with emotion.

"Hold!" snapped Tarbizon. "This could be a trick. There are humans working with the reen, you know. See if you can find out who it is."

The sage threaded his way up the narrow portion of stairs not covered by the upended cabinet and stretched over the top of the cabinet to get his mouth near the door. "Who is there?" he shouted. "Who are you?"

There was a quick muffled reply. The sage turned to stare down at Tarbizon. "He says he's a Peacekeeper, High Master! He says to open the door for the High Chairman!"

Armindor lowered the stool he was holding to chest level. "Ask him what has happened to the reen," he called to the man.

"What became of those ratlike creatures that were out there?" the sage bellowed, a hand cupped to his mouth. He listened to the reply, then looked at Armindor. "He said, 'We killed a lot of them and the rest ran away'!"

There was a spontaneous cheer from the sages, most of whom had clustered at the foot of the stairs, and they snapped their fingers in the old custom of the northern tribes, to show pleasure. Jilla joined them, raising her hands and snapping her fingers. I'm not going to die after all, she exulted. No one is!

"What do you think, Armindor?" asked Tarbizon.

Armindor shrugged. "Open the door. If it is trick, we all die sooner. If it is not, I can put this stool down and we can all celebrate."

"Some of you drag that cabinet away and open the door," Tarbizon ordered. "Open it slowly, and try to shut it again quickly if you see any reen."

Florn, Durvn, and another young man moved the cabinet away from the door. The sage at the door lifted the bar and cautiously tugged the door open a finger-width. He put his eye to the opening for a moment, then, with a joyful chuckle he stepped back and opened the door all the way. The sages at the bottom of the stairs saw that a throng of Peacekeepers in full armor and bearing shields filled the doorway. At this sight, there was another cheer, in which both Jilla and Tigg joined. Armindor lowered his stool to the floor.

The Peacekeepers moved aside to let a man through the door. Like them, he was in armor, but his armor was rich and ornamental rather than simply serviceable; the leather of the coat was dyed russet, and the rectangles of animal horn sewn to it had been stained red. A colorful cloth band held his pale blond hair in place, and his earrings and nose plug glinted with the red gleam of precious copper.

"It's the High Chairman," Tigg whispered to Jilla.

The High Chairman stood at the top of the stairs for a moment, surveying the blue-robed crowd. "Is High Master Tarbizon here, by any chance?" he called.

Tarbizon raised a hand. "Here, Your Greatness."

The High Chairman's face broke into a smile and he started down the steps. "I'm truly glad to see that you are safe, Your Wisdom. We found a number of dead sages up there when we came in! You seem to have had quite a bad time of things here, eh?"

"It was indeed," acknowledged Tarbizon, moving forward to meet him. "We did not expect to survive it. But how did you chance to come here with all these Peacekeepers, Your Greatness?"

"It was not by chance at all. We came because—" He paused and glanced about, frowning. "Who is that talking?"

Tarbizon pointed at the box on the table. "It is a spell from the Age of Magic, Your Greatness. It is teaching us the ancient tongue. We think it was to capture it and some other spells that the reen attacked the guildhall."

The nobleman stared at the box with wide-eyed interest. "A voice from a box! You sages certainly find some incredible things!" He shook his head in wonder. "Well, as I was saying, we came here because I wanted to find out more about these ratlike creatures. This afternoon, two of my Peacekeepers brought me the dead body of one they had found in Market Square, and I realized that what you and that southern sage had told me about the things was true. They also told me that the thing had apparently belonged to Councilor Leayzar, and I found that very thought-provoking, inasmuch as Leayzar had made such a big fuss about not believing in the creatures that he had convinced me not to believe in them!"

He glanced about and found a nearby table edge to sit on. "It was obvious to me that Leayzar was talking with two mouths, for he had said there were no such creatures and here he was apparently keeping one as a pet! I collected a number of my Peacekeepers and went to see Leayzar to ask him some questions. When we reached his home we found no one there, at first. Then we looked in the cellar and found Leayzar—dead! He had been shot in the throat with one of those tiny darts that southern sage had shown me. Furthermore, there was an opening in the wall of Leayzar's cellar that led into a narrow underground tunnel that looked as if it ran below the streets of Inbal."

The High Chairman paused a moment and shivered noticeably. "I did not like the looks of things, Your Wisdom, I didn't like them a bit. I realized that not only are these reen things real, but they do live here in Inbal as you and the southerner tried to tell me, and it was also obvious that Leayzar must have been in communion with them for a long time. My guess was that they killed him because he would no longer be of any use to them now—but what had they been planning together?" He grimaced. "Well, I thought I had better come see you and find out if that southern sage was still in the city, so I could talk to him again about the creatures. For some reason I decided to bring the Peacekeepers with me, thank Garmood! When we got here we saw that the door looked as if someone had been trying to chop through it. I smelled trouble, so we broke down the door and came in. We saw a dead sage lying in the hallway and another at the foot of the far stairs, and at least half a hundred of the rat-things trying to gouge their way through your cellar door. Some of them blew darts at us, but our armor and shields saved most of us, although I did lose one man who was struck in the face. But the rest of us waded into the creatures using our feet and our spear shafts as clubs, and after we'd killed a dozen or so of the things, the rest fled. So that's how we came to save you, High Master Tarbizon. Now, is that southerner still in Inbal?"

Tarbizon indicated Armindor, who had come to stand near him. "There he is, Your Greatness."

The High Chairman looked at Armindor with some surprise. "You don't look at all as I remembered you. Why are you wearing that brown cloak?"

"I have been in disguise and hiding, Your Greatness," Armindor explained. "Councilor Leayzar has been trying to lay his hands on me for moons, since that day I appeared before the High Council."

"Leayzar," grunted the noble angrily. "Well, you won't have to worry about him anymore. I want to beg your pardon, Your Wisdom, for not believing you. But I have no doubts now! I want you to tell me everything you can about these reen, and help me figure out how to protect my city against them!"

Armindor bowed. "It was in the very hope of doing just that, that I came to Inbal, Your Greatness. I have pledged myself to alert all the rulers of the lands and cities of the danger from the reen."

"I can help you do that," offered the High Chairman. "I'll have my scribes write up a proclamation about the creatures, signed by me, that you can show to other rulers in case they doubt you as I did."

Armindor bowed again. "That would be of great help."

At that moment a Peacekeeper stepped in front of him to tell the High Chairman something, and Tarbizon moved to the noble's side to ask him a question. Armindor stepped back and looked about until he saw Tigg and Jilla standing side by side and grinning at him a few paces away. He moved toward them.

"Well, everything seems to have worked out very nicely," he observed. "We don't have to worry about Leayzar anymore, and the High Chairman is going to heed our warning about the reen after all. We shall have to stay in Inbal a little longer in order to help him, but springtime in the north is a pleasant season. Things could be a great deal worse for the Magician's Company, eh?"

Tigg and Jilla grinned at him and he grinned at them. The war against the reen had begun, and humans had won the first battle.

About the Author

Author TOM MCGOWEN says: "I wanted this book to be a rousing adventure story, but in addition, it points out the importance of scientific knowledge and technology, and the need for tolerance and cooperation among intelligent beings, regardless of their differing life-styles, beliefs, or physical appearance."

An editor for many years, Mr. McGowen has written more than thirty books for young people. He and his wife live in Norridge, Illinois. They have four children and ten grandchildren.